"Eli...open your eyes...please..."

A faint flicker of his eyelashes and finally she could glimpse the pale blue of his eyes. Unfocused. She could see his pupils weren't dilated. Good. He coughed more and closed his eyes. He became still again, though continued breathing. She examined the cut to his forehead—just a small trickle of watery blood from the gaping wound. At least the icy water had constricted the open blood vessels and stopped any bleeding.

As the last bit of strength seeped from her, she begged him, "Eli, please, open your eyes. Wake up."

And he did as she asked. His eyes locked onto hers with a flicker of recognition. In that moment, she knew he would live.

His hand found its way to her face. "There are those brown eyes I've been waiting to see."

Again, that phrase that always brought so much peace.

What did it mean?

Jordyn Redwood is a pediatric ER nurse by day, suspense novelist by night. She pursued her dream of becoming an author by first penning her medical thrillers *Proof, Poison* and *Peril*. Jordyn hosts *Redwood's Medical Edge*, a blog helping authors write medically accurate fiction. Living near the Rocky Mountains with her husband, two beautiful daughters and one crazy dog provides inspiration for her books and she loves to get email from her readers at jredwood1@gmail.com.

Books by Jordyn Redwood

Love Inspired Suspense

Fractured Memory

FRACTURED MEMORY

JORDYN REDWOOD

HARLEQUIN® LOVE INSPIRED® SUSPENSE

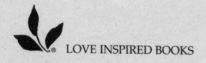

LOVE INSPIRED BOOKS

Recycling programs for this product may not exist in your area.

ISBN-13: 978-0-373-67766-5

Fractured Memory

Copyright © 2016 by Jordyn Redwood

Printed in U.S.A.

I thank my God upon every remembrance of you.
–*Phillipians* 1:3

For Kathy Springer. My longest and most dear friendship.

Acknowledgments

Every author knows no book is written in isolation, and this book was no different. Particularly this novel as it required me to write outside my comfort zone on a very short deadline. Thanks to Laurie Kingery, Lisa Carter, Candace Calvert, Casey Herringshaw, Liz Solan and Norma Mai for providing insight, edits and overall support as I navigated my way through the Blurb to Book contest. Thank you to Karl for providing law enforcement insight (as always).

To my agent Greg Johnson—
thanks for always being there when I need you.

Also, heartfelt appreciation to Emily Rodmell and all the Love Inspired editors for your interaction in the Blurb to Book team forums that definitely helped me write the best manuscript I could for a genre I needed to learn a lot about. I've truly been welcomed into the Harlequin family with open, loving arms. Most of all, I want to thank fellow book addicts. Without you, none of this would be possible and I'm always happy to connect with you via email at jredwood1@gmail.com.

ONE

The blank stare in Julia Galloway's eyes confirmed Eli Cayne's worst fear.

She didn't remember him. The amnesia had erased every moment he'd spent ensuring that she would live after the Hangman nearly claimed her life.

"Julia Galloway?" he asked, his voice husky with undeniable emotion at seeing her for the first time in eighteen months. The feelings he thought he'd stomped into submission surfaced with a vengeance.

Julia reflexively raised a hand to cover the scars where the rope had carved into her skin. "Who are you?" The ringlets of her blond hair dripped water on her black T-shirt and red plaid pajama bottoms.

Eli held his badge at her eye level. "I'm U.S. Marshal Eli Cayne. May I come inside? There's a matter of great importance I need to discuss with you."

Doubt washed over her beautiful face. Even if

she didn't remember the attack, the lingering fear was evident.

He showed her the manila envelope he held in his other hand. "Our office has received information that there has been a hit ordered—on your life."

She clenched the black fabric of her shirt tight into her other hand, her knuckles pale under the pressure. "Excuse me?"

"Someone has compiled a profile of information about you for a hit man to use to kill you. I'm here to get you to a safe place. Please, can I come inside?"

At first, the engine accelerating was distant until the screech of tires brought the hairs on Eli's neck to attention. Instinct propelled his hand forward, hard into Julia, pushing her into the foyer. A bullet whistled past his ear, shattering a picture frame directly behind the remnants of her silhouette.

Julia landed flat on her back on the hardwood floor. Eli delivered a swift kick to the door, throwing it closed and turned to lock the dead bolt. He fell to his knees at her side. Her eyes were wide with fright, and her mouth gaped open as she tried to draw a breath.

"You're all right. You just got the wind knocked out of you." He pulled one of her hands to his chest. "Slow, easy breaths."

Another bullet crashed through her front picture window. He had to move her to a safe place.

As Eli scooped her up, his fingers caught in the tangles of her long, wet blond hair. He carried her up the staircase just a few steps shy of the front door. Higher ground would be his only advantage in this fight against an unknown enemy. At the crest of the stairs, three doorways confronted him. He shouldered through the first one on this right.

A bathroom. No windows.

He swung her around and pulled the shower curtain aside resting her in the bathtub. "Stay here."

Julia shook her head. "No." Her brown eyes held more defiance than her whispered response.

"Stay here," he ordered. "I'm locking this door. Don't open it until you hear me say the words *red daisies.*"

He pushed the lock closed on the door and yanked it behind him, testing the knob once to make sure it was secure. He drew his weapon and crossed the hallway into Julia's bedroom.

"Shots fired. I need backup," he whispered into his wrist mic.

His FBI liaison, Ben Murphy, sounded distant—out of breath. "I'm in foot pursuit of the subject's car...trying to get...a license plate. Local PD notified."

Good. Knowing extra help was on the way left Eli free to accomplish what he needed to do to

protect Julia. He couldn't assume the rest of the
house was clear. The number of assailants that
could be after Julia was unknown. Was someone
lurking in her home now—waiting for the perfect
opportunity to attack?

He hugged the wall of her bedroom. It was
clean and uncluttered. There was a computer desk
with a bookshelf above adorned with several tro-
phies. Competitive swimming if he remembered
correctly. A Bible lay open on her bed, pillows
piled high against the headboard.

Slowly, he slid open the door to the master bathroom and noted soapy water in the tub. He'd interrupted her from a soak and quiet time. Backing
out of the bedroom, he entered the other room. A
spare bedroom. The closet clear.

Back in the hallway, he faced the stairs. So far,
Julia had followed his direction. The door to the
bathroom remained closed. He eased by and took
the stairs in cautious increments. At the bottom to
his left was a small dining room. A quick check
showed no one hiding under the table. To his right
was a small sitting room. Shards of sprayed glass
glittered in the early-morning light as the curtains
waved in the soft breeze. In the distance, the faint
sound of sirens approached his location.

Eli faced the hallway toward the back of the
first floor with the TV room and kitchen. From
the fruity aroma he guessed she was brewing tea

even as the color of her eyes reminded him of the rich chocolate brown of coffee.

Those eyes…

He shook his head to clear the image.

Focus.

Distraction was always the first nail in the coffin of a law enforcement officer.

The pantry was clear. Single-car garage with an older-model white SUV. No one underneath. He opened the door to her backyard. Small, quaint. No high trees or shrubs that could be hiding a suspect. Cheerful flowers edged the neatly cut grass with garden shoots just venturing up from the warmed spring ground.

He reentered the house and went back to the front door, surveying the yard. Nothing seemed out of place. Even though the concussive sounds of gunshots still rang in his ears, they hadn't drawn a single curious neighbor from their home. Not one eye peeked out from behind closed curtains. Was everyone at work already? He turned back around and closed the door.

Time to check on Julia and release her from the small bathroom he'd locked her in.

He pocketed his weapon. Into his mic, he said, "Ben, what's your location?"

"Walking back to the house. Lost the suspect. Description of vehicle and partial plate sent to local PD."

With one foot on the stairs he looked up only to see Julia with a revolver aimed straight at his head.

Julia sucked in a breath. If only she could stop her heart from beating so fast. Her chest ached.

"Who are you really?" she asked.

Either Eli was who he said he was or he was posing as the good guy to cover his true intentions. His pale blue eyes narrowed at her question; he was clearly contemplating what explanation he could muster to keep her from pulling the trigger.

He kept his hands visible and still. "I *am* a U.S. Marshal. Eli Cayne. I showed you my identification."

"I barely got a look at it before someone shot at me." She squared her shoulders and adjusted the aim of her weapon. This was what she had practiced. What she always prepared for. She had rehearsed this scenario over and over until she hardened her mind to ignore her heart if she really had to kill someone.

"At us." Eli pointed his thumb to his chest. "I was right here, too. Those bullets could have found me just as easily."

"A law enforcement ID can be bought."

He raked his fingers through his chestnut hair before settling a thumb and forefinger on his stubbled chin. "Julia, if I wanted to kill you I would have done it already. Right when you answered the door."

"You could be working with someone."

"You're right. I could. Can you hear those sirens? They're awfully close. Why would there be help on the way if I was the killer? Did you call them?"

Her shoulders relaxed, and she eased the weapon down a bit. The sincere look in his eyes became more convincing than her resolve to shoot an intruder.

"At some point, you're going to have to trust that what I've said is the truth. I'm here to keep you safe."

Julia lowered the revolver. "Red daisies?"

"What?"

"Those were the best safe words you could come up with?"

Eli's relieved smile solidified her impression that he couldn't truly be nefarious. "I had to think of something on the spot that a killer wouldn't say. It was the best I could do."

She pointed the weapon to the floor. Her eyes darted to the side as a fist pounded her door.

Eli raised a calming hand. "That's my partner on your case, Ben Murphy. Are we good here? Can I let him in?"

She motioned to her pajama pants. "I'm not entirely presentable."

"Get dressed and then come down. There's a lot we need to talk about."

Julia backed away from the top of the stairs and closed her bedroom door behind her. She crossed the room to her closet and pulled out a pair of jeans and a floral turtleneck. In the bathroom, she brushed through her wet hair. Her hands still trembled from the massive adrenaline release.

What she wanted back was the peaceful morning she'd planned. After three hard days as a nurse in the pediatric ER, especially after losing a child from drowning, she needed some quiet to recoup.

The gunfire shattered the solitude she so badly needed. Had the horrors she'd already survived come back to haunt her? What was it about Eli that tugged at the erased threads of her mind? There was something about him, his presence, which felt warm and homey—like hot chocolate on a cool autumn evening. In the wake of her parents' death, it was a feeling she craved.

There was a three-month gap in her memory starting from the time of the attack until she entered rehab for a brain injury caused by a lack of oxygen at nearly being hung to death. From the subsequent brain swelling, Julia had been in a coma and on life support for a month. Then, according to her grandfather, she'd spent another two months in the hospital until she grew strong enough for a rehab facility. Her remarkable recovery had astonished doctors, who were convinced she would never be anything other than persistently vegetative.

Julia's first memories were shrouded in a foggy sea where she relearned to eat, walk and speak. Even now, nearly two years after the incident, there were only fleeting moments when Julia could sense memories from those three months trying to break through the imprisonment of her brain injury.

Six months after her near murder, the Hangman's trial started.

Julia didn't follow the news threads about the trial. The prosecutor chose not to have her testify, as her fractured memory was of no use to his case. The forensic evidence the Hangman left behind was enough to seal his fate.

Even though her mind was healed, she had to convince everyone else she was all right. The Colorado State Board of Nursing insisted she complete additional testing and clinicals to ensure that she was competent enough to practice nursing.

Almost two years of her life given away to a criminal. For her own sanity, she had made a conscious choice to not make attempts to retrieve the lost time, suppressing her normally inquisitive nature to avoid everything on the internet about the man who tried to kill her—a doctor who had been a coworker.

Someone she had once called her friend.

Now that she had started back nursing in the

pediatric ER, all she wanted to do was heal kids and stamp out disease—as they always said at work.

Had that been wise? Did her lack of knowledge about the Hangman and his crimes put her at a disadvantage now?

She quickly dressed. Running shoes seemed to be the best option for a day where she had already been shot at before nine o'clock in the morning. From the stairwell, male voices snarled like lions arguing over territory, but as soon as her feet hit the landing, they stopped.

Eli broke through the trio of uniformed officers and led her to her kitchen. He pulled a chair out for her. Another man, dressed in a charcoal-gray pinstriped suit, followed him.

"Julia, this is my partner, Ben Murphy. We'll be working together on your case. He's from the FBI."

The FBI and the U.S. Marshals working together?

Ben reached his hand out to her. "I wish we could have had a calmer introduction."

His hand enveloped hers. Strong grip. His black hair, longer and swept off to one side, stood in stark contrast to his emerald-green eyes.

"Nice to meet you, Ben." She sat in the chair, pulling her hand from his.

Ben continued. "Since the Hangman's case was under federal jurisdiction because of the Wyoming murder victim in his series, your death threat was forwarded to us by a local parole officer. However, FBI staffing issues provided an opportunity for us to work with the marshals, who are more skilled at protecting witnesses. We bring different assets to your case."

"Tea?" Eli asked.

She nodded.

"Pumpkin spice creamer and two teaspoons of sugar?" Eli stated more than asked.

Her lips pursed. How did he know?

He went directly to the cups and pulled one from the cupboard. No riffling around the kitchen in a blind search.

Electrical currents pulsed through her chest. He knew where they would be.

How was this possible?

"I see you're getting low on your stockpile." Eli shook the container to emphasize his point and examined it closer. "No matter, it expired two months ago." He pulled out the trash drawer and chucked it in.

He not only knew her but knew her home.

"Who are you?" Julia demanded.

He turned to her, cup and spoon in hand, stirring her concoction slowly. "Eli Cayne. Marshals—"

"No." She held her hand up. "Who are you *to me*?"

He crossed the kitchen, set the cup down in front of her and turned to his cohort. "Can you give us ten minutes?" Ben handed him the manila folder. The one Eli claimed marked the end of her life.

Eli unbuttoned his suit jacket, and she noted dark patches on the broad expanse of his tailored shirt. Water from her hair, from when he had carried her up the stairs. Something about being held in this man's arms had felt so strangely familiar. Comforting. Julia pushed the thought aside and watched as he lowered himself into the chair across from her. She gripped the cup between her hands to cut the fear-laden chill that set in her bones.

"I used to work for the Aurora Police Department. I was the lead detective on your case. I've only been with the marshals' office for about a year and a half."

How much did she want to know about their past? Had there been anything besides a professional relationship between them? Pins and needles rushed over her body. She felt light-headed. Fear rose within her. The daily battle to keep it at bay faltered.

Julia placed her palm on the envelope and slid it on the table between them. "Tell me about this. Tell me why you're here."

Eli pinched the flimsy metal clasp together, pushed the flap open and pulled out the documents. He fanned the pages out, turning them around so she could see them. "This is what we call a hit package. It's typically put together by some-one who wants to hire a hit man for murder. It has all the pertinent information of your comings and goings. Photos of your house. Your vehicle and its license plate. Your gym. Place of employment…"

His insistent litany became distant in her ears as she gathered up the pages. The details of her life laid out like a scrapbook for a killer. Her sched-ule. Where she went grocery-shopping. Where she volunteered. A picture of her grandfather and his assisted living center. Had her papa been put into danger because of her? Her throat tightened—her turtleneck like a gloved hand around her throat. As much as she loathed wearing it, the collar hid what she could not confront.

"Who is this person?" Her voice broke from clenched vocal cords.

Eli sighed. "At this point, there doesn't seem to be an obvious candidate. Dr. Heller, who mur-dered several people and nearly killed you, is on death row. This is a copy. The original is in evi-dence. We're examining it to see if it will give us clues as to who this person might be."

"Where did it come from?"

"It was given anonymously to a local parole officer who then delivered it to the FBI. Can you look at these pictures of the other victims? We never found a strong tie between them and you other than a health-care background. Do you know any of these women?"

Julia glanced at the photos. Some did seem vaguely familiar, but none that she knew by name. She straightened the pages and handed them back to Eli. "I'm afraid I can't help you. I don't know if you're aware, but I suffered a brain injury as a result of the hanging. I have post-traumatic amnesia. Any memories from the time of my attack until I went into rehab are gone. The next months are fuzzy and..." She brushed the tears from her eyes. Why did something she couldn't remember traumatize her so deeply?

Eli covered her hand with his. Familiar again, unnerving yet protective at the same time. How could one touch be all those things?

She cleared her throat and continued. "I was sick for a long time. I've just gotten things back to normal. If there is such a thing after what I lived through."

"Julia, what's important right now is to get you somewhere safe. When we do that, hopefully we'll have time to figure this out."

Hopefully? His words didn't instill confidence. The threat was serious and even he didn't conclusively sound as though he could keep her safe. Was he depending on her remembering something she couldn't?

"What are you asking me to do?"

"I'm asking you to come with me. We're placing you in protective custody until we find the person who wants to kill you."

TWO

Julia pulled two suitcases from underneath her bed and laid them open on top of her hope chest. In that chest were many things she treasured from people close to her who had died. Her mother's journal. Her father's old baseball glove. Patchwork quilts her grandmother had sewn for great-grandchildren she would never know. Eli slid the Bible toward him and placed his index finger on the highlighted text.

"'Fear thou not, for I am with thee. Be not dismayed, for I am thy God. I will strengthen thee. Yea, I will help thee. Yea, I will uphold thee with the right hand of my righteousness.' Isaiah 41:10."

Julia stilled and watched him smooth his hand over the crinkled pages. It unnerved her to hear his voice read something so intimate. Was he reading the notes she scribbled in the margin? Her most closely held thoughts? Those pages were worn with overuse. How often had she read this verse to herself to change her heart?

To help her believe that God could provide peace from the fear and worry that plagued her.

How could she get the Bible back without seeming to be trying to hide something from him?

"Do you believe in God?" she asked, holding out her hand.

He closed the Bible gently and held it out for her. "I do, but I have to admit I'm a little jealous."

She pulled the book from his hand. "Of me? Why?"

"You seem…intimate…with those words."

Ben, who had been leaning against her door frame, walked to the center of her bedroom. "Julia, you can't bring anything that could potentially disclose your location. No cell phone. Nothing electronic. No computer. E-reader. We can't take any chances."

Julia put the Bible at the bottom of her suitcase. "How many days do you think I'll be gone? I need to notify the hospital. I need to tell my grandfather something so he won't worry."

Ben neared her. "You can't say anything that might give a hint that you're being put in protective custody. Tell your grandfather you're leaving on vacation and won't be available by phone for a few days."

"But I call him every evening."

"You can't," Ben insisted. "Not for a while. I know it seems harsh, but it's as much for your safety as it is for his."

Eli eased Ben away from her with a nudge to his shoulder.

"Julia, I don't want you to worry about your grandfather," Eli reassured her. "I'll personally ensure his safety. The marshals' office will have someone keep eyes on him, as well."

"Is there any other close family we should be concerned about?" Ben asked.

Julia turned away and walked to her closet. She couldn't bear saying it. That she was alone in the world. Her parents were dead. No siblings.

"Ben, let me worry about Julia's extended family. Like you said, this is my area of expertise."

Had Eli said that to protect her from having to talk about her lack of a family? Did he know all about her past?

"Also, we'll need a cover story for the hospital," Ben said. "Perhaps you could tell them your grandfather has had a medical emergency and you need to go on a leave of absence. You don't know when you'll be back."

With several items of clothing in her hands, she turned back to face them. "You have no idea how long I'll be gone?"

Eli was the one who met her gaze. "We'll try and resolve this matter as soon as we can, but we can't give you a time frame. I'm sorry."

"Can I have a few minutes alone?"

Eli motioned Ben out of the room. "Let's give her some space."

"I need to make some calls," Julia said.

Eli nodded and closed the door behind him.

Julia neared the window that looked out over her backyard. She didn't want this to be her life— to be forced to run when she finally found some measure of peace and purpose again. But hadn't that been what she was doing psychologically by not attempting to fill in the pieces of those missing months? This was just the physical expression of what she'd done mentally for a long time. She had struggled to let the past be the past. Now it pursued her, and she wasn't prepared to handle what could happen. And what piece of the puzzle did Eli hold? How did he fit?

She picked up the phone. "Papa?"

"Dear Julia. It's early for you to be calling."

Her grandfather's voice calmed her nerves. "Papa, I don't want you to worry, but I won't be able to call for a while."

"Why? What's happened?"

"It's not something I can talk about right now. Please, just know I'll be in good hands."

"Is everything all right? I don't like how vague you're being. It's not like you to hide something from me."

The tears fell freely. How her heart ached to not be able to disclose what was happening to the one man who'd given her everything. "It's been a rough few days."

"How so?"

"A child I took care of died. We couldn't save him."

"How did he die?"

"He drowned in a hotel swimming pool."

"If only you could have been there to pull him out. You were a great lifeguard. No one died on your watch."

What her grandfather said was true. If only every parent knew CPR. A child in these modern times shouldn't die of something so preventable. There was a point of no return despite all the advances of modern medicine. Julia knew—she had almost been there. "It was just too late by the time he got to us."

"I'm sorry. I know you take it personally when a child dies. Your heart is so big, Julia, but though you feel upset by this incident, that's not what's really going on."

"I promise to tell you someday soon—just not right now."

"I'll expect a full explanation." Her grandfather's law enforcement background would let him be appeased.

"Yes, sir."

"I love you, Julia. Don't ever forget that."

Her chest heaved. She bit her lip, and tears rushed down her cheeks. She hadn't realized Eli had entered her room again until he sat on the bed next to her, and the movement tilted her body into his side.

He brought his arm up around her shoulder. "I'm going to get you through this, Julia. I promise. I'll take care of your grandfather. Nothing will happen to him."

And somehow she felt it wasn't the first time he said those words.

It always surprised Eli how nondescript safe houses looked. This one was a town house in a middle class neighborhood. He parked in the driveway and got out. Julia didn't immediately follow him.

Best to give her some time to absorb her surroundings.

He went around to the trunk and removed her two suitcases. As he rounded the car to the passenger side, she ventured out, edging her car door closed. He motioned her to follow him up the porch steps. At the door was a key code lock. He punched in a few numbers and entered, holding the door open for her.

"We change the code at the beginning of every week," he said. "We feel it's more secure than having a key floating around." Directly ahead was a staircase. "The only thing down here is the garage entrance and the utility closet. Everything else is upstairs."

Eli waited for her to climb the steps. Cautiously,

she stepped as deliberately as a cub exploring beyond his mother's boundaries. At the top, he motioned to the left. She took the lead and opened the door. He scooted in behind her and rested the suitcases at the bottom of the bed.

"There are cameras in every room but the bathroom." He pointed out the one in the corner. "We'll generally leave you alone, monitoring you through the cameras. I'm going to give you this." He pulled a balled chain from his pocket that held a white square with a prominent red button.

"My grandfather wears one of these."

He held it up, and she dutifully bent her head forward as he laid the chain over the turtleneck. A soft tendril of her hair slid over his fingers, stirring a warm memory. Eli forced himself to stay on task. This woman's safety was the only priority. "It's essentially the same thing. I'll let you decide if you want to wear it under your shirt or not."

She clasped her fingers around it. "I press it and you're here at my whim?"

Her smile was timid but unexpected heat surged through his chest. "Within minutes, someone will be here. Preferably me."

"How does this work?"

"You'll be monitored twenty-four-seven by a team of agents. We don't want to be obvious to the neighbors, but their response time is a couple of minutes if they see anything concerning or you feel like something is out of place."

"I should unpack?"

"Do what feels comfortable to you. We don't want you to feel like a prisoner." He handed her a sheet of paper. "This is the phone number for the agents who are monitoring you when I'm not here. This number won't change, so I suggest you memorize it. If you want to go anywhere, they'll take you."

She took the slip of paper from his hand. "You're not staying today?"

Relief swept through him. Was it possible that she saw something in him she remembered? Or was it just merely that he'd been there to save her life this morning?

"I'm going to leave you with Ben tonight as I follow up on forensic items from the hit package, and I'm going to pay a visit to your grandfather. I had a few grocery items placed in the kitchen that should get you by until tomorrow."

"Thanks for everything you're doing, Eli."

"I've upended your life. I'll try to make the transition as easy as possible. There are a few things I want to go over with you, since this hit man seems to prefer bullets." Eli leaned against the dresser. "If we're in a car getting shot at, I need you to get as low as you can."

"Wouldn't that be natural instinct?"

Eli smiled. "You would think so until it actually happens to you. People tend to freeze in a crisis, but your emergency nursing background probably won't allow that happen. You're trained to work through that—to fight instead of run."

"One thing in our favor."

"Julia…" His voice trailed, his eyes distant. "If you're ever taken hostage, the best thing is for you to work with us to try and get free. Try to keep the assailant's head in clear view."

For a kill shot.

"Do something. Anything. Drop your weight unexpectedly, but whatever you decide, just give me a warning before you do."

"Like what?" Julia asked.

"We'll keep the words *red daisies* as a code. For just you and me—okay?"

"You think someone could actually get in here?"

He shook his head. "It's unlikely, but we try and plan for all contingencies."

"I'll see you—"

"In the morning. What time are you usually up?"

"I work day shift, so I'm used to being up by five thirty."

"I won't wake you before then."

He turned to leave, trying to squash the thought of taking Ben's place over the next few hours. If he didn't solve the mystery of the hit package, Julia Galloway would never be safe.

Julia began to unpack her clothes into the plain, unvarnished pine dresser that sat in the corner.

How many other people placed their belongings here? Did all of them live through their experience? When she pulled the drawer open, pen-gouged letters in the bottom of the top drawer read...

I was here. Kristin.

Worry. That was what this statement meant to Julia. This person wanted something permanent to mark her existence. A note that someone would read to imprint the memory of her in their mind.

How frail human existence was. Another lesson from the medical trenches.

I will remember you, Kristin. Who will remember me?

Loneliness overwhelmed her. An ever-present ache in her chest that was hard to stymie. Her fingers trailed over the front of her Bible. The words inside were the only reminder that she was never truly alone.

Hugging herself, she knew she wanted more. Physical contact with someone who loved her. God meant people to be in relationship with one another.

Her life...her history...meant isolation.

Nothing could change what she'd already lived through, but neither did she feel it was good for things to remain the same. It had felt unexpectedly natural to be in Eli's arms—she wanted to have that feeling again.

Julia had decided to pack a week's worth of

items and wash them if her exile extended beyond that. Five pairs of jeans. Ten pairs of socks. Some items it was best to have extra of in case the worst happened.

That was another lesson of the ER—always prepare for the worst-case scenario.

Next came the stack of short-sleeve shirts. Long-sleeve shirts. Plenty of scarves. Three pairs of pajamas.

Her gun sat at the very bottom. Julia glanced around the bedroom, trying to find the best place for it. She tucked it underneath the mattress and then stowed the suitcases in the bottom of the closet.

After everything had a proper place, she ventured into the kitchen. Ben sat at the two-seat kitchen table, his laptop open in front of him. He seemed lost in thought—his gaze drawn to the view of the children's play equipment that backed up to the town house, a small park for families that lived close by.

Children played while their watchful mothers stayed nearby. Several boys threw mulch chips at one another. She cleared her throat. He broke his gaze and turned her way.

"All settled?" he asked, closing his laptop.

"As well as can be expected."

He rose from the table. "Can I get you anything? I think Eli put some tea in the cabinet."

"You sit. I don't want to disturb your work."

Julia walked into the kitchen and began to scour the cabinets. She found several boxes of flavored tea. On the stove top was a stainless steel teakettle. She lifted it and filled it with water. "Can I make some for you?"

"I'll try anything once. Coffee is my go-to beverage."

"You know, I never got the taste for coffee, which always surprises people when I tell them I work in health care."

"That does strike me as odd."

"How do I make a long story short? During nursing school, I worked with a hospice nurse. When we were visiting a family after her patient died, they offered me a cup."

"I take it that didn't go over so well?"

Julia chuckled. "It was the strongest, most bitter liquid I'd ever put in my mouth, but I drank it because I didn't want to appear thoughtless. From then on—"

"No coffee for you."

Not to mention that the aroma of the coffee had also been forever linked in her mind to the stench of death. Julia shuddered and turned the water off, set the teakettle on the stove and turned on the gas burner. "Exactly, just tea. So, what is it you do for the FBI?"

"I guess you could call me a jack-of-all-trades. My specialty is computer forensics, but I hated being cooped up indoors, which was part of why I joined the FBI—to get to work in the field."

"And outside of work?"

"I know I don't look the part of the rugged mountain man, but when the snow is melted and the sun is out I'm usually hiking. Evergreen is home."

Julia tapped her fingers on the counter as she waited for the water to boil. "Have you seen the insane gymnastics maneuvers people are attempting these days? I didn't even know what parkour was until some kid came in with a broken arm after trying it."

Ben laughed. "Those parkour people are a totally different breed. A little—" he whistled and circled his finger next to his head "—cray-cray to say the least."

"Do you have children?"

His lips parted slightly as if to speak and then clamped down. A flash of unhappiness appeared in his eyes as quickly as it was replaced with a placid smile. "No children."

"Sorry if that's too personal, but that phrase you used is common with kids these days, and I noticed you watching the boys in the park."

He crossed his arms over his chest. "I'm just keeping a close eye on the perimeter. The agents outside don't have a view of this side of the property. I'm curious though. What's it like? Working with kids all the time?"

"Challenging. You can have the best and worst moment in the same day."

"How is that possible?"

Julia pulled two cups from the cupboard. "I've saved a child's life and lost another in the same day."

Ben placed his elbows on his knees. "What's it like for you to lose a child? As a nurse?"

Julia's pulled down one of the boxes of tea Eli had stocked. It touched her that he'd gathered these for her to try and make her feel more comfortable. There hadn't been a man in her past who had even tried to be attuned to her needs. "I can't speak as a mother about the loss of a child, because I've not been one, but I know as a nurse to lose a patient...particularly someone so young..." Julia pressed the back of her hand to her mouth. Her gut clenched. There had been too many lost little ones in her eight years of nursing. "It's devastating."

Contemplating her statement, Ben shifted back and looked out the window.

There was something there. Something hidden she couldn't quite figure out. Years of nursing instilled in Julia a wealth of intuition. Every day, she had to interpret the things patients could not say.

A child claiming her black eyes and swelling lips were the result of running into a door. The teenager with small, deliberate razor cuts on her forearms as the only means to experience the pain she could not speak of. It was her expertise to read the smallest impressions of verbal tone, the slightest shift of body language that would disclose a truth a patient didn't want to confess.

She placed a tea bag in the brown mug.

Ben settled his eyes back to her. "I've lost victims in the line of fire. You're right...it's tough. But it's not like losing a family member."

Julia's parents came to mind and how she didn't have them anymore.

Ben was right—it wasn't the same.

Eli slowly walked up the steps of the one-story redbrick structure of the facility where Hank Galloway, Julia's grandfather, was a resident. His thoughts often wandered back to Julia, how seeing her in the flesh, so strong and healthy, made it difficult to keep his emotions in check.

In law enforcement, it was rare to see a good outcome to someone who had suffered from such a violent crime. Knowing that Hank was a retired law enforcement officer, Eli figured it would be hard for him to keep his nose out of Julia's business—particularly if he felt her life was in danger.

Eli's goal was to make it clear to Hank that that was exactly what he needed to do to help ensure Julia's safety.

As he entered the facility, he spied the U.S. Marshal who was working undercover dressed as a volunteer to help keep an eye on things. They acknowledged each other only with the briefest glance as Eli approached the receptionist's desk and inquired about Hank's room.

She pointed down the hall. "Third door on the left."

Eli inhaled deeply. He undid the top button of his dress shirt, loosened his tie and tried to dismiss the vexing nature that the fading imprint of holding Julia in his arms had on him. He knocked softly, semihoping that Hank might be napping.

"Enter." The voice was strong—anything but weakened with age.

He stepped inside. On the wall hung several commendations and awards from Hank's law enforcement career. They locked eyes, Hank's brown eyes, so similar to Julia's, clearly sizing Eli up.

"Well, if it isn't the prodigal son."

Hank, a few inches shorter than Eli, struggled to plant his cane and push himself up from the rocking chair.

Eli crossed the room quickly and grabbed his forearm to steady his tremors. Parkinson's disease had ravaged his body and laid waste to his muscles. He was a hunched-over remnant of the man in the photos.

"Sir, please, you don't have to get up."

"I always like to meet a man eye-to-eye. Particularly one who took such an interest in my granddaughter."

Holding tightly on to Eli, Hank struggled to

a standing position and clasped Eli's hand in his strong, chafed, leathery one. Even though his other muscles were weak, the ones in his hand were seemingly spared from the ravages of the disease.

"I know you were the detective on Julia's case. Recognize your face from the newspaper stories but you're also the one who helped with her rehab. Or am I just being presumptuous?"

"Guilty as charged."

"Nice to officially meet you, son. I'm Hank Galloway."

"Eli Cayne, sir."

"Now sit down," Hank ordered.

Eli assisted Hank back to a sitting position and grabbed a folding chair that sat against the wall.

"I take it your visit has to do with Julia's strange call earlier today."

"It does, sir."

Hank muted the game show he'd been watching and began to rock in his chair. "I noticed a new volunteer working today. Does that have to do with you, too?"

"It does, sir."

"But you're not going to tell me what's going on?"

Eli sighed and settled his back against the cool metal of the chair. He eyed the door. The less Hank knew about Julia's situation, the better off he was, but Eli also knew Hank's bloodhound genes wouldn't let him sit idle—Parkinson's or not.

Maybe just letting him in on the secret was the best way to keep him from trouble.

"The U.S. Marshals' office is concerned that a hit has been placed on Julia's life. I've placed her in protective custody."

The chair creaked as Hank pushed it back and forth for a good minute, his eyes never leaving Eli's, the squeaking like voltage up Eli's spine.

"So you're with the U.S. Marshals now."

"Yes, sir."

"I don't have much in the way of financial reserves, but I'd like to give you some money to offset the costs from all the help you gave Julia."

Eli lifted his hands up. "It's not necessary, sir. I was honored to be able to help."

"Seems unusual for a man to take such interest in a girl and not want anything in return."

And there it hung in the air between them. It was time for Eli to verbalize to this patriarch that he never had any ill intentions as far as Julia was concerned.

Eli smoothed his palms over his legs. "At first, after rescuing Julia, I wanted to know if she was going to live. Being the one to find her that close to death—you can't help wondering if you were there in enough time."

"And then when that was clear?" Hank asked.

"Then Julia became the one person who could

maybe tell us who this evil man was. When it was obvious that she was having difficulty remembering, I thought the stronger she physically became, the more likely she would remember. Helping with some of her rehab expenses, and spending time with her—encouraging her to get stronger—gave me the opportunity to continue to question her and test her memory."

"All that time you spent with Julia, and yet we never met face-to-face...were you intentionally avoiding me?"

Eli smoothed his hands over his face. What answer would be the most reasonable? What answer wouldn't make him seem like some creepy stalker? "I was worried about the case. I was worried that the defense could use my involvement in Julia's rehab as a way to say the whole case against the Hangman was tainted. That I was wrongly influencing her. The more family members I interacted with then the more likely I could be accused of being improper so I did make myself scarce when you were around. What was most important was getting the Hangman off the streets. When Julia's memory improved to the point that she was remembering things day to day but that the details of her attack were lost—I thought it was the best time to bow out."

"And that was the only reason? To protect the case?"

"That was the only reason."

Hank Galloway lifted an eyebrow—his built-in lie detector alarming.

Even to Eli, it didn't feel as if he'd completely told the truth.

THREE

Eli parked his car behind the two agents who watched Julia overnight. His heartbeat picked up slightly. There was no denying he was anxious to see her again. He was excited to tell her the hit package had revealed a set of fingerprints they were hoping to get a match on. Thus far, the parolee remained elusive.

Exiting the car, Eli approached the other agents' vehicle. A navy blue, older-model Ford Granada—in fact, the first type of car he drove as a teenager.

He used his knuckles to tap on the window. Will Sullivan and Jace Bastian looked his direction. Will sat in the passenger's seat with the laptop of the security feed from Julia's town house. Jace took the opportunity to exit the vehicle and stretch his legs. As he opened the door, two large McDonald's coffee cups tumbled onto the broken pavement.

"How'd the night go?" Eli asked.

Jace pushed his hands toward the sky, a groan

escaping his lip. "Nothing exciting to report. She read, she slept. Still sleeping."

Eli glanced at his watch. It was almost nine. Julia said she was an early riser. Perhaps the stress of yesterday had taken its toll. It was a plausible explanation.

"Last contact?" Eli asked.

"By phone around nine o'clock last night. She was asleep an hour later," Jace said.

"What about Ben?"

Will looked down at his laptop. "He's not visible on any of the camera views."

Intuition fired through Eli's mind. "Call Julia," he ordered.

"But she's sleeping," Will said from inside the car.

"I don't care. Call her. Get her up."

Eli rounded the car, opened the door and ripped the laptop from Will's hands. Jace had the phone up to his ear. Eli could hear the phone ringing through the miniature speakers.

Julia didn't move.

Will shrugged. "Maybe she's a heavy sleeper. I'm telling you—Nothing. Happened."

"That's the problem." Eli circled his finger in the air. "Call her again."

Jace rolled his eyes and with dramatic flair dialed Julia again. Eli would address the tone of those movements when he wasn't scared something had happened to Julia. This time, she did stir. Eli exhaled. On the feed, he could see her grope for the phone on the bedside table.

Her movements were stilted...clumsy.

Taking the laptop with him, Eli grabbed the phone from Jace in the moment Julia answered the phone. "Julia?"

Breathing. No words.

"Julia—are you okay?"

Was he overreacting? Perhaps she was a heavy sleeper and he'd hastened her from bed the one morning in a long time she was sleeping in. Stress. Being hunted by a killer could definitely sap a person's strength.

"Hurts..."

He looked back at the laptop feed. She was sitting up rubbing her hand against her forehead. No, not the right words. She was barely able to hold herself upright. Her body would drift to the side and she would jolt herself back into a sitting position.

"Are you sick?" Eli asked.

She slumped backward on the pillows. "Bad headache."

He pulled the phone from his ear and set it against his chest. "Will, was she drinking last night?"

"Tea—"

"I mean liquor."

Will laughed out loud. "Julia doesn't strike me as one who imbibes."

On the screen, Julia's arm dangled off the bed and she dropped the phone. Eli shoved the laptop and Jace's phone at Will. "Call 911."

"And tell them what?"

"Give them the address. Tell them it's a medical emergency."

Eli's feet pounded the pavement with Jace's footfalls close behind him. Trees rushed by as he pumped his hands faster to get his legs to pick up speed. Nothing looked disturbed from the distance as he rounded the corner and nearly pummeled the door as he dropped his speed. He jabbed the key code into the lock.

It didn't release.

He tried again.

Nothing.

"It's Monday. The lock's code has changed," Jace said with his hands on his knees as he huffed from the short sprint.

"Get it." Eli seethed.

Jace patted his pockets and held his hands up empty. His phone was in Will's possession. Eli reached for his and keyed in his code and handed it over to Jace and then began to pound on the door. "Julia!"

"I got it. I'm sure she's fine." Jace entered the code.

The door released, and Eli almost tripped over Ben's body crumpled at the base of the staircase. He kneeled down and placed his hand in the middle of Ben's back. "Ben! Can you hear me?" Ben groaned in response and tried to lift his hand up, but it immediately flopped back down. "Jace, carry him outside for the medics."

Eli raced up the staircase and straight into Julia's bedroom.

She remained in the same position he'd last seen her in on the computer screen. Eli sat next to her on the bed and grabbed her shoulder. "Julia. Julia!"

Julia shook like a rag doll under his touch. He licked his finger and placed it under her nose. A faint wisp of breath crossed his finger. He pinched the muscle between her neck and shoulder as hard as he could—a trick from his police days to see if an unconscious person could be roused.

Nothing.

Glancing around the room, nothing seemed out of place. A cup of clear liquid was the only other thing on the table next to her bed. He took a quick sip. Definitely water. No pill bottles.

Will came through the doorway. "What's going on?"

"Did Jace get Ben outside?"

"Yes, but he's not waking up. What's wrong with them?"

"I don't know." Eli lifted Julia's limp body. She was a deadweight in his arms. His throat tightened. Immediately, his mind raced back to the moment he'd cut the rope from around her neck,

catching her lifeless body as she fell into his arms.
Her skin…so cold and pale. How his breath seized
in his chest that he'd been too late to save her.

Just as it did now.

Lord, you cannot do this to me again.

He carried her to the couch, where EMS would
have more room to work.

Eli teased her eyelids open and examined her
pupils. They seemed normal size—not the dark
black holes of the dead or drugged. Julia still
didn't move. The subtle rise and fall of her chest
the only evidence of life.

At least this time she was still breathing.

There was something off about her appearance.
For bed, she'd dressed in light black cotton pants
and a pink T-shirt. He traced his fingers over the
scars on her neck and felt her pulse. Something
in his mind begged him to remember. Her lips. It
was the color. He brushed his thumb over them,
spurring his memory into action.

His job was to observe. To catalog every detail to determine if something was amiss. After
she'd packed and dressed yesterday, she wore little
makeup. Her lips had not looked this red.

Unnaturally red. Cherry red.

He brushed his thumb against her lips again.
Definitely not lipstick.

Voices called out as he heard heavy boots racing
up the stairs. Two paramedics in their firehouse
bunker pants and suspenders eased him back.

"What happened?" one asked. Eli took in the name on the badge. Russell.

"She complained of a severe headache, seemed unsteady and then passed out. I can't get her to wake up."

Another firefighter surveyed the living room.

"Is someone helping my partner, Ben? He's unconscious outside."

"Yes, another team is with him. What's her name?" Russell asked.

"Julia Galloway."

"Age?"

"Twenty-nine."

"And you are?"

"Eli Cayne."

"Relationship?"

What could he say? Protector?

Eli indicated himself and Will. "We're U.S. Marshals."

That raised Russell's eyebrows. He turned away from Eli and focused on Julia. His partner snaked his hands under her T-shirt and attached heart monitoring leads to her chest, a blood pressure cuff to her arm and a lit probe on her finger. Next came some oxygen delivered through small tubes in her nose.

Russell placed a fisted hand in the center of her chest and rubbed it against her sternum. "Julia? Julia! Can you hear me?" He took a penlight from his pocket and shone it into her pupils. "Equal and reactive to light," Russell noted. A firefighter helped the paramedics by documenting Russell's findings.

Russell's partner called out, "Vital signs are normal. I'm going to start an IV."

Russell turned back to Eli. "Do you know anything about why she wouldn't be responding to us? Did she fall and hit her head? Did she take any drugs or alcohol that you know of? Is she a diabetic?"

"No, no, and I don't know."

Russell turned to his partner. "Let's get a blood sugar. After that, let's try a dose of Narcan."

"What is that?" Eli asked.

"Narcan is a medication that reverses narcotic drugs if people overdose on them. The blood sugar will tell us if she's diabetic."

At that moment, a piercing shriek filled the small townhome. Everyone startled and Eli reached for his weapon.

Julia didn't flinch.

"What is that?" Eli yelled.

A firefighter bent over and pulled the contraption out of the plug. The alarm ceased. "Just as I thought. It's the home's carbon monoxide detector. Found it on the floor. There are toxic levels in this place."

Russell snapped his fingers in the air. "Everyone…go, go, go! Let's get her outside."

Eli reached under and scooped his arms under

Julia's and lifted her up. Russell grabbed her legs. It surprised Eli how quickly Russell could go down the stairs backward with a body in tow, but he was likely used to doing it every day.

"Straight to the rig, guys," Russell instructed, and they raced Julia to the back of the open ambulance door.

A second ambulance screeched to a halt in the street just behind the two fire trucks.

"Hey," Russell yelled to his cohorts. "Get that guy loaded fast and on one hundred percent oxygen. There's a carbon monoxide leak somewhere in that place."

One of the firefighters held a thumbs-up sign and began to scoop up Ben's lifeless body.

Eli and Russell clamored up the two steps at the back of the ambulance and plopped Julia down on the narrow gurney.

"Are you coming?" Russell asked Eli.

"Yes." Eli saw Will and Jace hovering by the front door of the townhome. "Jace! Meet me at…"

"Sage Medical Center," Russell said.

Jace nodded, and Russell yanked the doors closed and pounded on the roof. After that, he busied himself removing the oxygen prongs from Julia's nose and placing her on an oxygen mask. Eli heard the rush of air as Russell cranked the oxygen to its maximum flow rate.

Eli sat on the bench opposite the gurney and

grabbed Julia's lifeless hand. "Is this all from the carbon monoxide?"

"Likely. It explains why both of them fell ill."

Eli shook his head as scrambled thoughts scurried through his mind. "What does that do to a person?"

Russell placed a blue tourniquet around Julia's forearm. "Carbon monoxide is a toxic, colorless, scentless gas. It replaces oxygen on your red blood cells and starves the body of oxygen. That's why she complained of a headache. Your brain gets very cranky when it doesn't have enough oxygen."

"Why didn't we get sick?" Eli motioned his hand between himself and Russell.

"It takes time for that process to happen—about fifteen minutes minimum if the levels are high. Once you open a door, the gas will start to vent out. We didn't have enough of an exposure to be symptomatic."

"Can you treat it?"

Russell withdrew the needle from its plastic sheath and then shoved it into the back of Julia's hand. Drops of her blood hit the floor of the ambulance before Russell could connect the IV solution. Her life spilled out in front of Eli. Was he at fault? Could he have prevented this from happening?

Russell pointed to the mask. "The oxygen. If it's really bad, the doctor may place her in a hyperbaric oxygen chamber."

"Will she be all right?" Eli asked.

"If we got to her in time, she'll be fine. I just don't know if we're in that window."

For the first time in a long while, Eli bent his head and prayed to a God he'd distanced himself from.

Lord, keep Julia safe. Heal her body.
I need her in this life with me.

Under the muffled sound of sirens, Julia's eyelids fluttered open. Her head...pounded, the surge of blood like freight trains rushing through a cross stop. She tried to pull her hand to her forehead to put counterpressure against the pain, but something snagged her hand.

Warm fingers swallowed her hand up. "Julia."

Eli's voice. Strong. Concerned. She inhaled a calming breath. Everything would be okay if he was with her. Why did she feel so terrible? Her body ached worse than when she contracted the flu. With her other hand, she groped her face and felt the mask covering her mouth and nose. The oxygen cooled her face. When she tried to pulled it off, another hand pushed it away.

"Leave it on, Julia." Eli again. "You're in the back of an ambulance."

Blinking several times, she tried to clear her blurred vision. She tried to sit up, only to be stopped by the strap around her chest. She was covered by a rough, well-used cotton blanket.

Julia shook her head to try and clear her thoughts. "What happened?"

Eli gripped her hand tighter. "They think it was carbon monoxide poisoning."

At first, it didn't mean anything to her. Even her medical mind couldn't process the information. Everything was so jumbled. Fuzzy.

Then a stranger's voice. "My name's Russell. I'm a paramedic. Glad to see that you're waking up."

Her eyes finally focused. Eli's blue eyes softened. A faint smile came to his lips. Her heart ticked up a notch.

"How did it happen?" Julia asked.

"What?" Eli said.

"Julia, are you allergic to anything?" Russell asked.

She shook her head. "Accident or on purpose?"

Confusion clouded Eli's face. How could she make him understand what she really wanted to know? Had this been an attempt on her life?

Russell interrupted before Eli could respond. "Do you have any chronic illnesses? Do you take any medications?"

Julia shook her head again. "Did they try to—"

Russell's head loomed into her field of vision. "Julia, I think it's best if you rest. Your confusion is normal. Once we get the poison out of your system, you'll start to feel a lot better." He patted her shoulder and sat back down.

"Kill me?"

Eli gripped her hand in both of his and bent his head, resting his forehead against her fingers. Her heart sank as tears fell down her face, collecting in her ear wells.

He didn't know. He couldn't answer her. But his posture spoke of defeat. Eli was strong. Smart. Maybe even the kind of man she dreamed might someday take an interest in her. He was trained to prevent crime—to pick up on circumstances that were suspicious. She could tell he felt responsible for what had happened.

When he looked up, his blue eyes held hers. Fierce. Determined. "I don't know if this was deliberate yet, but I'm going to find out."

If Eli Cayne couldn't keep her safe…could anyone?

FOUR

Eli was relieved that after six hours of hyperbaric oxygen therapy, Ben and Julia were fully awake and seemed back to themselves, though bored at being cooped up. Ben was medically cleared and officially discharged from the emergency department. Eli ordered him to go home and rest for the remainder of the day. He found Julia in the next room flipping channels on the small screen mounted in the corner of her room. She had dodged a bullet again. At least figuratively this time. Eli had made a quick trip back to the town house to get her a change of clothes and her Bible. Anything he could do to provide her comfort he was willing to do. In the short twenty-four hours since they had been reconnected, there was one attempt on her life…now two?

He and Will stood in the hall outside Julia's room. Will looked better than Eli felt after Eli insisted he head home and grab a few hours' sleep. Since they were a man down on Julia's detail, Eli needed him back sooner than later. Will sidled up next to him and looked in through the window. "She looks good. Are you going in or just hovering?"

"I haven't decided yet."

"Do you want the good news or the bad news first?" Will asked.

Eli adjusted the grocery sack in his hand that contained the items he'd collected for Julia. That was always a loaded question as far as Eli was concerned. "Good news first."

"There was a crack in the furnace. That town house was built in the eighties. Who knows if the furnace was ever replaced? According to Quentin, that safe house hasn't been used in years."

"That's the good news?" Eli adjusted the bag in his hands. "I can't wait to hear the bad news."

"FBI Forensics thinks it may have been tampered with. They're not hanging their hats on it yet, but they are dusting for prints and having some other analysis done to see if they can prove it out."

Eli turned to Will. "How are we supposed to get Julia to trust us? The first night she's in our care she nearly dies."

Will smirked. "Come on, Eli. That might be a little bit of an overstatement. Look at her now—she's perfectly fine. I overhead one of the nurses say she could be discharged home today like Ben."

Eli shook his head. "No, not today. I want her

here until we can thoroughly check out the next safe house. Two agents—one inside her hospital room and one outside."

"If you insist."

"I do. I'll be having a discussion with Quentin. It's his responsibility to ensure that these locations are thoroughly vetted before the witness arrives. Having a witness die while under the protection of the U.S. Marshals would bring horrific embarrassment to the agency."

Will held a hand up. "Eli, I get it. I know this is bad. But are you sure there's nothing more? Even though it's not the FBI's main focus, witness protection is not a walk in the park. The very nature of protecting people is rife with problems."

"Your point?" Eli asked.

Will stuffed his hands into his pockets. "You don't seem to be handling this well. I'll admit— it doesn't help her trust us. It makes us look bad, but she's okay and we'll do better next time. In reality, I'm not sure how we could have prevented the furnace issue." He paused and rocked back onto his heels.

Or how could we have kept someone from tampering with it? Isn't that the more appropriate question?

Eli felt it in himself—the tight tension he didn't know how to dispel without lashing out. What was really going on? On the surface, Will was partially right. Protecting a witness was a mine field and he should manage these issues with a calmer head, and he usually was very levelheaded. With Julia, his protective instincts were in overdrive. Was it more than preventing her death? Was it that he had this strong emotional attachment that tethered his mood to her level of safety? The more her life was at risk, the more unsettled and angry he became? That wasn't the most rational response for someone just doing his job. If the FBI proved tampering, that would mean her killer had discovered the location of the safe house and accessed it before their arrival.

That changed everything.

It would indicate someone paid a lot of money to track Julia down even in protective custody. Or someone involved with inside knowledge leaked where she was going to be.

Simply pulling Julia from her normal routine might not be enough. A mole put her life significantly more at risk. Was it even possible?

The truth was, seeing Julia limp and lifeless this morning had been too close for him. Too close to the moment when he'd held her the last time and she barely clung to life. If he didn't get these feelings that had simmered for over a year stuffed back into containment, he wouldn't be able to do his job.

Eli shook his head to dispel these thoughts.

Eli—pull yourself together. Don't let your feelings for her put her at risk.

He cleared his throat. "I owe you an apology."

"It's all right."

Eli squared his body to face Will's. "No, it's not. You're right. I haven't acted in a professional manner."

"I've talked to Quentin myself on this matter and he gave me the location of the next safe house. I agree with you she's safer in the hospital overnight. They're getting ready to release Ben as we speak. I'll go to the next location with a maintenance man and make sure all utilities are working properly as well as the security systems. Furnace check. Fire alarms. Carbon monoxide detectors in place."

"Thanks, Will. I appreciate your work on this. Let's be thorough. There are worse things than keeping her tucked here for a few days."

"Exactly. I'll head out and work on those details. And you?"

Eli shrugged and held the grocery bag up. "I guess I need to work on building her trust in us again."

Julia couldn't find anything to watch on TV. The headache and chest pain were gone, and the latest blood result showed the carbon monoxide was cleared from her system. She was free from the confining hyperbaric oxygen chamber. Why hadn't she been released as the doctor said she would be?

What disturbed her were the visions…or hallucinations…or could they be actual, real memories?

In some ways, her amnesia was a blessing. There wasn't the terror of knowing exactly what happened to her on a daily basis. The subconscious remnants were what plagued her and likely were the cause of her anxiety. Would working to recapture those memories heal her from the anxiety? Was she brave enough to try and do it?

Today, she remembered more than she ever had before about the attack.

At least, she was fairly certain that what she remembered was true.

On that fateful day, Julia had just come downstairs after getting ready for work. She was about to put on her brightly colored paisley clogs that were tucked under the table in her foyer but decided it might be best to get her lunch ready instead. There had been the softest click and a cool breeze that swept through her kitchen. She'd crossed over to her sliding glass door to see if she'd left it cracked open from the previous evening. Peeling aside the curtain, she could see it was latched. Even the security bar was down.

When she turned around, a man stood just feet away from her. Even recalling this much caused her heart to fire indiscriminately, and she checked her pulse to see if the rhythm was regular. Resting her head against the pillow, she closed her eyes.

Why can't I see you? Why are you just a fuzzed-

*out figure? I locked the front door. How did you
get in? Has my mind made this whole thing up?*

What was new was seeing a figure at all. Was
it something to be celebrated? Julia wasn't convinced. After all, if it really couldn't offer any
new information, what good did it do her except
cause her more anxiety?

Then what replaced it was the sweet singsong
of a male voice that whispered to her. *Those are
the brown eyes I've been waiting to see.*

The faint knock at the door caused the memory
to vanish. Eli poked his head into her room, and
she motioned him forward.

The second thing that caused her anxiety? The
gap in her memory claimed every moment she'd
interacted with Eli. Considering the things he
knew about her, it reasoned they'd spent a lot of
time together.

"You look a lot better," he offered, pulling
a chair closer to the bed. He set a thin plastic
grocery bag at her side. "I brought you these. A
change of clothes and your Bible."

She grasped the bag with the tip of her fingers
and pulled it closer. "Thank you. I can't wait to
get out of here."

His eyes darted to the side. "That's what we
need to talk about."

"I don't want to stay here."

"You're safe here. I think it's—"

"No! Eli, please…" She pressed her thumb and

forefinger at the corners of her eyes to stem the flow of threatening tears.

He rested his hand over hers. "Julia, it's okay. You're a nurse. You practically live in a hospital."

How could she explain it to him? Was it the environment that was culling these memories? Was it being in the same position, forced to stay in a hospital bed that was connecting her brain cells again? Or was it Eli's presence?

She fisted her hand and rested it at her side. The truth of the matter was her psyche was unprepared to remember the attack.

"Julia, I can only help if you tell me what's going on. Like all men, I'm a really horrible mind reader." He took her hand and gently uncurled her fingers, smoothing his palm against hers. "One night is all I'm asking. We want to be sure the next safe house doesn't have any maintenance issues." He gently squeezed her hand to add strength to his request.

"You don't think the elevated carbon monoxide levels were an attempt on my life?" Julia asked.

A brisk knock at the door, and Dr. James Solan entered. His hazel eyes glimmered under the light nearly as much as his bald head. "I thought you said to me once you'd never step foot into an adult ER again."

Eli stood from his chair. "You two know each other?"

"I worked here for about two years after I graduated from nursing school until I figured out adults were too crazy for me."

Solan stroked his white beard. "It was obvious she didn't like to care for anyone twenty-one and over. She'd bargain with the other nurses to take care of their pediatric patients." Looking at Julia, he stated, "You don't know how much they miss that."

Julia laughed. "Sadly, it took me a couple of years to figure out there are hospitals that exist where adult patients aren't allowed. Don't know how smart that makes me in the long run."

Dr. Solan turned to Eli. "Don't let her fool you. She was one of the best nurses we ever had. As much as she'd hate to admit it, her adult nursing skills were above par." He turned back to Julia. "As I'm sure they still are if you'd ever like to come back."

"Not unless I can't find any other job."

"I'll never give up trying to win you back. Julia, is it okay if I discuss your medical information in front of this young man?"

Eli held a hand up. "It's okay, I'll step—"

"It's fine, Eli. Stay."

"Very well, then. I know the nurse relayed to you that your last carbon monoxide level was negligible. The good news about CO poisoning is that if it's caught early enough, patients turn around very quickly and don't suffer any long-term effects." He motioned to Eli. "I understand from the

EMS team that this gentleman here found you. His quick action likely saved you from having a serious medical fiasco."

Did she just see Eli blush?

"You're medically clear to go home when you're ready."

"Thanks, James," Julia said as he backed out of the room. "It was good seeing you again."

Eli returned to the seat next to her and shook his head. Was it relief at the doctor's words? The closer she examined Eli, the more she noticed his state of distress. His hair was disheveled. The blue irises tinged red. Had Eli not slept well? His face was one of worry.

"I want to go back to the question you were asking me before the doctor came in. They found a crack in the furnace at the safe house and the FBI is looking into the possibility that someone may have tampered with it."

Blood roared in her ears. Could this assassin have found her that quickly?

"Julia…" His voice trailed, and he looked away. There was something he wanted to tell her but he seemed to question if whatever truth he held could be too much for her to take. Eli lifted his eyes. "Do you trust me?"

Unexpectedly, his question felt like a punch in her gut. In every relationship, there was an inherent amount of trust. Just based on her position as a nurse, she expected her patients and their families to trust her on some level in order for her to do her job. If a family didn't have that basis of understanding, it made her care more difficult because the doubt they possessed clouded every action she took at the bedside. Did that nurse clean my child's skin enough before she put the IV in? Is that why my child now has a blood infection three days later?

Eli locked her eyes with his. "I can't do my job unless you trust me on some level."

"Why do you think that I don't?"

"I'm just putting myself in your shoes. I uprooted you from your life, and the first thing that happens is you almost—"

"Eli, I don't blame you for the furnace. How could I?"

His body relaxed. "I'm relieved, but I also would understand if you'd want another agent to take my place."

Julia found herself shaking her head before her mind registered a thought. If she was truthful, she would have to confess that she wondered if Eli could keep her safe, but there was also a feeling that she didn't want to be separated from him. "I don't want that. I don't want to have to get to know another team. I want to stick with you and Ben."

For now.

FIVE

The next morning, Eli was hopeful for an uneventful day. Will and Jace reported there had been no overnight incidents at the hospital. Ben was well rested and relieved the two of them so they could sleep.

Eli was parking his car in the hospital lot when a call from Quentin redirected him to this location—the house of a murder victim. Quentin insisted Eli drive to the crime scene without seeing Julia first. Aurora police provided backup for Ben until Eli could get there.

No. This isn't possible. This can't be happening again.

The fact of the matter belied what Eli hoped. The woman was dressed in a sharp-looking turquoise and black pantsuit, her longer auburn hair covering the bulky rope around her neck that had claimed her life. Suicide? Homicide? One black, high-heeled shoe was on the floor below her. The other dangled from the tips of her toes.

Quentin Archer, Eli's supervisor, waved him over. A tall black man, he stood nearly six foot five—a good three inches over Eli. His voice was James Earl Jones deep and he always presented a stabilizing force in any situation he was involved in—even when bullets were flying. Though he exuded polite calm and unflappability—the job had aged him beyond his fifty-four years. His hair was gray and the beard he wore fashionably clipped barely held the color of his youth.

Eli and Quentin stood off to the side as Aurora police detectives began to analyze the presumed crime scene. Eli waved to Nathan Long, a well-respected detective he'd had the honor of working with on occasion. Local law enforcement would handle the case, which added to Eli's apprehension as to why Quentin called him to the scene.

"Quentin."

"Eli, thanks for coming by."

Eli motioned to the woman. "Not that you gave me a choice. What does this mean for Julia?"

"That's what we're here to discuss and why I wanted you to see the crime scene for yourself. You understand my concern?"

"I see a woman who may or may not have committed suicide."

"Follow me."

They rounded to the backside of the woman's body. Quentin pointed to the noose. "What we know about the Hangman is he is very methodical in the way he dispatches his victims. Each noose had a device that was anchored into the ceiling. The rope—always yellow nylon. The noose was elaborate—far beyond what was needed to kill somebody. Decorative, you could say. The perpetrator would need to be skilled in tying knots."

"Like the doctor currently on death row for the Hangman's crimes. Have they found any blood?"

"The man who was convicted of being the Hangman, Dr. Heller, was a pediatric intensivist and doesn't have the skill that, say, a surgeon would have with tying knots." Quentin smoothed his hand over his mouth, his eyes narrow. "And no—so far they haven't found any blood."

Eli shrugged. "If it proves to be murder, perhaps we have a copycat at play. The Hangman's trial was televised and heavily covered by the media. There was extensive forensic presentation of the materials he used to make the noose and how it was anchored."

"Perhaps." Though Quentin sounded far from convinced. "From looking at the scene right now, how could it possibly be suicide? There is nothing under her feet she could have stepped off of."

That was problematic. Eli's gut tightened. "Who is she?"

"Evelyn Roush was CEO of Medical Interventions International or MII. They're a company based out of Colorado Springs."

Eli fiddled with the coins in his pocket. That

was concerning. All the Hangman's victims had a connection to the health-care field. As of yet, they hadn't determined if the medical angle was significant or just the killer's preferred type.

"What does the company do?" Eli asked.

"From what I gather, they revolutionize life-support equipment. Recently, the company was in the news for getting FDA approval for a specialized type of ventilator. Evelyn just became infinitely richer than she was before—quadrupled her net worth."

"I'm sure Aurora PD will look at all the usual suspects. Husband—"

"She wasn't married. No kids. Early reports say she dedicated her life to her company and was also a big philanthropist."

This woman's death, on the surface, could be connected to Julia, but there wasn't a logical straight line. If it was the hit man—why a hanging and not bullets? And if the real Hangman was free and not awaiting a state-sponsored injection to whatever was beyond this life—why didn't he choose to kill Julia in the same manner as before?

Quentin sighed and nudged Eli from the room with his hand pressed against his back. He didn't stop guiding Eli until they were in the front yard. Eli put his sunglasses on—in part to shield his eyes from the sun, but also to hide his feelings from his more experienced, astute supervisor.

"I know you were involved with the Hangman's

case. I know you were part of the responding team that found Julia barely alive. How did that come about?"

"What?"

"That you found Julia?"

"The hospital called and reported her missing after they tried to get a hold of her for two hours when she didn't show up for work. I was in her neighborhood when Dispatch notified us of the need for the welfare check. It was the same day—"

"Of the high school shooting."

"I wasn't tasked on that case, and I knew it would be hours before a uniformed officer would be available, so I decided to stop by and help out. Get it off the call log."

Eli turned away from Quentin. He could feel the emotion of that day building in his chest. What he thought was going to be a quick safety check had changed his life forever. When he'd gone up her steps, there was no answer at the door. When he peered through the side window—he saw her. Much in the same fashion he'd just seen Evelyn Roush.

"It's good for Julia that you were so close."

Eli squared his shoulders and turned back to Quentin. "Are you accusing me of something?"

"Should I?"

"Absolutely not."

Quentin put a firm hand on his shoulder. "I don't think you're the Hangman. I am concerned you might be too emotionally connected to Julia—finding a victim that way, barely clinging to life, resuscitating her and perhaps developing feelings—"

"I don't have feelings for Julia Galloway. I was just doing my job then. *Am* doing my job now."

A knowing look crossed Quentin's eyes.

Am I so easy to read?

"What I see is that, perhaps, your judgment is clouded. Even though there is a man in jail serving for the Hangman's crimes, we should consider the possibility, in light of today's event, and the hit on Julia's life, that the Hangman was not working alone."

Eli's mouth dried. Was it possible? They had missed a partner all along? "If that's true, then why is this person killing again? He could have walked away scot-free after Mark Heller's conviction."

"What it suggests to me is two possibilities—a seasoned serial killer who can't help himself or someone with a personal vendetta against this group of people, and he's not going to stop until his sense of justice is satisfied."

Did either of those possibilities carry the same threat against Julia?

"Then why hire someone to kill Julia? Why not finish her off the same way he tried to before—especially considering this murder."

"That, Agent Cayne, is what you're going to have to figure out."

"Get me access to Mark Heller," Eli said.

"You want to interview the Hangman?"

"You're implying he didn't act alone. I think an interview is warranted."

"What's his incentive to open up to you?" Quentin asked.

"Heller has always claimed his innocence."

"As they all do." Quentin smirked.

"True—but if he offers new information and this crime ends up being linked to the Hangman, he'd be in a good position for appeal and ultimately getting his freedom back."

"You're prepared for what that means for you—personally and professionally?"

Eli's stomach clenched. Could he have put an innocent man in jail? Or had he just let a partner go free?

Either possibility wasn't acceptable.

Julia relished her friend Crystal's smile. It had been too long, since before her attack, since they'd had a chance to catch up.

"I got a heads-up through the hospital rumor mill that you were down here in the ER, so I snuck in under the guise I was your nurse. I'm glad I wasn't shot on sight for doing so."

Ben lifted his eyes briefly from his laptop. "I might reconsider next time."

Crystal winked at him and turned her attention back to Julia. "I'm so glad you're not mad at me for not being there for you when you were so sick."

"How could I be now that I know your mother was going through cancer treatment. I'm so glad she's okay."

Glancing around the room, Julia was unnerved to have Ben sitting in the corner listening to their private conversation. He tried his best to be non-obtrusive, but the more Julia watched Ben's face, the more she felt he was hiding something from her. Frequently, he placed his finger against his earpiece listening to communications, which often was followed by a slight frown. A few times he'd stepped out of the room to talk with the agent outside her door. And where was Eli? He'd told her he'd be back at the hospital this morning. So far he hadn't shown up and it was nearly ten o'clock.

Ben didn't present the same type of peaceful calm that Eli did. There was an undercurrent of something smoldering that she couldn't quite put her finger on. Home problems? Ben said he didn't have children. Perhaps he couldn't have any. Julia eyed his hand. There was a simple gold band on his left fourth finger. Today, he had a nervous energy about him—like a kangaroo hyped up on caffeine. But then, he'd had the same brush with death that Julia had. Perhaps that was enough to explain his behavior.

The curse of nursing enveloped her. Why

couldn't she just enjoy people for who they were? When did the analysis of people stop? The issue with emergency room patients, at times even their parents, was that they didn't always tell the truth.

What she needed to learn was that not everyone was hiding a lie, either.

"Julia…" Crystal's voice trailed as her face tilted toward the ground. Her long, wavy brown hair dropped over her face.

Julia reached for her friend's hand. "What is it? I want this to be a happy time together. Anything to keep my mind off what's going on."

"I feel so bad talking about my mother when your parents…"

Both died. That was the line her friend couldn't finish. Was that really why she hadn't heard from Crystal since her attack?

"It's okay," Julia offered.

"On their way to the hospital to see you." Crystal broke down. All Julia could think to do was place a comforting hand on her shoulder until the sobbing subsided.

The truth was Julia had suffered more loss than she thought humanly possible. Each day was a step into unknown territory. Before her attack, she'd parroted the same response to friends that everyone said to her.

Don't worry. God won't give you more than you can handle.

That was a myth perpetuated by people in good

faith but poor understanding. The Bible was rife with people getting hefty doses of more than they could handle. What was the purpose of suffering? What Julia learned was that at the point where life became overbearing—that was when the only option left was to throw your hands up to God and let Him take over. It was in a human's ultimate weakness that God's strength poured through.

Which left her saying, "I was never really alone. God was with me."

Crystal lifted her eyes. "I wish I had your strength."

Julia shook her head. "That's the thing. It's not my strength. I was so weak that I had to let God take over."

Her friend shook her head, wiped away the tears, but smeared black lines across her cheeks. "How is that possible?"

Waterproof mascara was a must for ER nurses. Perhaps it was different for those who worked in surgery.

Julia was about to answer when something on the television caught her eye. The headline in white lettering with a red backdrop, Has the Hangman Struck from Prison?

"Crystal." Julia grabbed the box of tissue next to her bed and handed a few to her friend. "I don't know how to answer. I just pray...a lot." She offered her a smile. "Do you mind if we meet for tea sometime soon? I'd really like to get a little sleep."

Crystal patted her eyes dry. "Of course. I'm being so selfish—"

Julia grabbed her hand. "No, you absolutely aren't. Please, don't think that. You've been a bright spot to my day."

Her friend reached for her from her chair and hugged her. "Whatever it is you're going through might not be so bad if you have all these handsome police officers keeping track of you."

Julia caught Ben's smile from the corner. He really was listening.

"One day I'll tell you why they're watching over me. It's not as glamorous as it looks."

As soon as Crystal left the room, Julia dashed out of bed. She paced to the closet and yanked the flimsy grocery bag from the bottom of the locker.

Ben stood from his chair, nearly knocking it over. "Julia, what are you doing?"

"I'm leaving."

She upended the bottom of the grocery bag and spilled her clothes onto the bed. One thing that could be said about Eli was that he didn't know how to match women's clothes—at all. A pair of magenta pajama bottoms and a lime-green T-shirt with an autumn scarf tumbled onto her crumpled bed linens. *Seriously?*

"You can't do that," Ben stammered. "You're in protective custody."

"Am I under arrest?"

"No, of course not."

"Then I'm leaving." She yanked the privacy curtain around her bed. "And if you open this, it's not going to be pretty."

His shadow hovered on the other side. "Where are you going? Why are you so agitated?"

Never did she dream she could dress so quickly. She whipped the curtain open. Eli had forgotten a pair of shoes and socks. No phone, of course. Her wallet was likely still at the safe house.

Julia fumed and pointed at the television with the tantalizing, media-driven hook blazing across the screen. "Instead of asking me why I'm so upset, perhaps you could enlighten me as to what's going on. Is this what you've been hiding from me?"

"What makes you think—"

And in that moment, Eli pushed through the door—pair of shoes and socks in hand. He glanced between Ben and Julia, his lips pressed together.

Julia grabbed the shoes from him. "Thank you, Eli. You read my mind."

"What's going on?" Eli asked.

Ben pointed a thumb at her with a look in his eye that screamed *toddler having a meltdown in the middle of a grocery store.* "She says she's leaving."

Julia placed her hands on her hips. "And you, Eli Cayne, are not going to stop me."

Eli placed his arms wide as a peace offering.

"Like I said before, Julia, you're not a prisoner, but we do need to accompany you wherever you go."

"I don't need you."

The words caught in her throat. She wanted to pull them back. Eli's eyes softened. She had hurt him—even though she hadn't meant to.

"Please, just sit for a minute." Eli eased the chair away from the bed.

She plopped herself into the seat her friend Crystal had just vacated. "What aren't you telling me?" she asked Eli, tears spilling down her cheeks.

"I've told you—"

Julia pointed to the TV and it took the briefest moment for the information to seep in before his eyes registered an understanding.

"I'm not keeping anything from you. We don't know if this woman's case is connected to yours. The media make their living on speculation."

"So you don't think the Hangman is still out there?"

Eli stepped closer to her timidly—like a lion tamer to a newly acquired jungle animal. "I don't know, Julia, but what is your plan exactly? If it's possible that this is the Hangman and there's also the hit package that we believe threatens your life—you're going to manage this on your own?"

Her head fell into her hands. It was just like before. She wanted to manage her problems alone, but she couldn't…she always needed someone else. Why was this lesson so hard for her to learn? What was God trying to teach her?

She reached for the tissue and blew her nose. "Fine. What's your plan?"

"A new safe house. I'm here to take you there."

"I want someone to check my grandfather."

"Already done. I assigned an additional agent to keep watch over him."

She put on her shoes and stood up. "Then let's go. Seems like I'm nothing more than a sitting duck here."

"True, but maybe I should get something else for you to wear. People are going to think you escaped from the circus."

SIX

Julia felt the SUV rock forward as Eli closed the tailgate after placing Julia's suitcases in a vehicle not her own for the second time in forty-eight hours. Life with Eli was an adventure to be sure. He rounded to the driver's side, got in and buckled up.

Jace sat behind her in the backseat. Ben and Will were following in a vehicle behind them—for ultimate safety, Eli assured her.

Julia hyperextended her fingers. The satisfying pop did little to settle her nerves. There was something she needed to tell Eli. Not that she didn't want to tell him—she just didn't know if it was a good idea to mention it when he had so much on his mind.

The gun she packed was missing. It wasn't underneath her mattress when she went back to the town house to pack.

Surely, there was a good explanation. One of the agents likely found it and had stripped it from her the way they do when suicidal patients come into the ER. They likely thought it better if they assumed total ownership over her safety rather than let extenuating factors undermine their efforts. It was better to trust those you knew and had experience with under stressful situations. Even though Julia was an ER nurse, none of these agents knew her skill set or could anticipate how she'd act under pressure, because they'd never witnessed her actions under fire.

"Something wrong?" Eli asked.

Julia jumped, his words amplified like a megaphone into her mind. The words tumbled from her lips. "I had a gun at the safe house. It's missing." Truth was that Julia never had been good at keeping secrets.

Eli backed the vehicle out of the driveway. "That explains why you're so distracted."

Was he that good at reading her already? "I'm fine…really. A brush with death doesn't really faze me anymore."

Eli didn't laugh at her remark, though she intended it to be funny.

"Let me check with everyone to see if someone secured it. That's likely what happened."

"I didn't take the weapon," Jace offered.

"Good," Eli said. "One down, only twenty more to go. There're quite a few people that have been in and out of that town house."

"And if no one has it?" Julia asked.

"We'll have to report it missing."

Julia leaned her head against the window. "How far is this new place?"

"A couple of hours. Up into the mountains. Just outside Estes Park."

Julia closed her eyes. It was one thing she didn't do enough—spend time in the mountains. Springtime in the Rockies was beautiful. The melting snow coursed down the rivers bringing ice-cold water yet renewed life to the valley. Hibernating animals ventured from their winter dens. Estes Park was always rife with elk that held the right of way even over pedestrians.

Why didn't she spend more of her free time there? There was nothing tying her to the city. Was it the underlying fear of something she couldn't remember? Would she always feel this way—alone and scared? Perhaps more than she could even confess to herself.

Eli cleared his throat. "Julia, there's something I want to ask you."

His voice dropped a trace lower than normal. *Do I really want to know what he's going to ask?*

"Seems like we have a few hours to talk."

Julia glanced back at Jace, who tried to distance himself from their conversation by looking out the window.

"Is there anything more that you remember from your attack? Anything at all?"

Her breath quickened in her chest, and her body

tingled. Why would he ask that now? "Is there something you're not telling me?"

"About what?"

The sun dipped toward the horizon in the afternoon light. Julia dropped the sun visor. The beginnings of a tension headache caused her forehead to throb. "About the woman who was found dead today."

Eli tapped his fingers against the steering wheel. "What do you want to know? I already told you I don't think it's connected to your case."

"But you're not sure."

His fingers stilled. "No."

A simple statement that said so much.

"Is that why you're asking me? Because you think the wrong man is in jail?"

Eli stared straight ahead with the vigilance of a sniper zeroed in on a target. "I hope not. I don't think so. The evidence against Mark Heller was substantial. Blood with his DNA was found at every crime scene. He had known affiliations with the first woman who died."

Julia nodded. Maybe it was time she stopped hiding with her head buried in the sand. "Will there be a computer where we go?"

Jace said from the backseat, "We can work to get you something that will be secure if you'd like."

"Why?" Eli asked.

"Did you know that I worked with Dr. Heller?"

"From investigating your case, I know the two of you both worked in the PICU. But were you more than that?"

"Not in any romantic sense, but I would have called us friends, which always made it hard for me to believe—" Julia's throat closed, cinching her voice.

"I get it. It's hard to imagine any friend would deceive you, let alone try to kill you."

Julia inhaled deeply. "If you had worked with him or seen him care for children, you'd never believe he was capable of doing the things he was convicted of."

"Tell me," Eli prompted.

Was this Eli's backdoor way of trying to unlock her memories? "There are physicians who have a Dr. Jekyll and Mr. Hyde personality. They're one way with patients, usually friendly and charming, and yet sickingly awful to the nursing staff. He was kind to everyone. Housekeeping. Unit coordinators. A very gentle personality."

"Everyone has a dark side," Eli said. "I've seen the mildest-mannered people do the most heinous acts. There's rarely the neighbor who says on television after the bodies are discovered, 'Oh yeah, I had that guy pegged to be a serial killer all along.'"

Jace laughed from the backseat. "That is so true, my friend."

Heat rushed Julia's face. "Dr. Heller wasn't that

way at all." *Why do I feel such a need to defend him?* "There was this little boy with Down syndrome we were caring for who needed a blood transfusion prior to surgery and he had the most rare blood type—AB negative. We were having trouble getting enough on hand for the transfusion, plus enough for his heart operation, and Dr. Heller directly donated his own blood for this patient."

Why was she trying so hard to convince Eli that Dr. Heller was a good person when all the evidence pointed otherwise?

"Yet he has confessed to having an affair with the first victim," Eli said.

"What's that supposed to suggest? That a man who steps outside his marriage is evil enough to kill? Everyone makes mistakes."

"Could it not have put his blood donation at risk? Sleeping with multiple people?"

Julia shrugged. What could she argue against the point? The affair didn't paint Heller in a positive light.

Their SUV swerved left over the double yellow line.

"Pay attention to the road," Jace said. "We can discuss pertinent matters of the case when we're all safe and sound."

"It wasn't me," Eli said.

"Sure," Jace replied.

"No, I'm serious."

Julia looked at Eli and could see the puzzled expression on his face. He leaned forward, looking at the dashboard. "No emergency lights on."

"Probably just a dip in the road," Jace said.

Julia hadn't realized how much time had passed. The road narrowed to two lanes. The river crisscrossed on either side of the road, its banks swelled with turbulent, frothy water. The young boy who had drowned popped into her mind.

"Setting aside how you feel about Dr. Heller, have you ever regained any part of your memory from those missing months?"

Was it time to confess the shadowy figure from her dreams? Julia felt the seat belt tighten against her chest, the car suddenly decelerating. She turned around and saw Jace grip her headrest. Ben's car, with Will driving, narrowed the distance quickly.

"Eli, seriously, what's going on?" Jace asked. "I'm about ready to fire you as chauffer and take over."

Even though Eli shrugged, the tense lines of worry that creased his forehead spoke more than his demeanor. "Something must be wrong with the car. Next town we'll pull over and get it checked out. Should have stuck with the old, faithful Ford Granada."

"Why didn't we take that car anyway?" Jace asked.

What unnerved Julia was Eli's silence.

* * *

There was something wrong with the SUV, and Eli couldn't make sense of it. He'd requested this vehicle because it was the newest, safest model on the lot, and now he wished he had old reliable back. Even before the car swerved over the median line and had the unexpected deceleration that almost caused Will to rear-end them—other things had happened he couldn't quite explain.

The radio and windshield wipers popped on without explanation. At first, Eli chalked up these minor happenstances to not being familiar with the vehicle.

Now he worried that all these things grouped together meant something more nefarious. The closest town was still twenty miles, and if something was happening that meant trouble, he didn't want the group stopping in the middle of this canyon on a two-lane road. Eli reached for his phone—just as he feared—no signal.

Ben's voice came over his earpiece. "You guys all right up there?"

How could he convey his worry to Ben without cluing Julia in that something more than mechanical difficulties were happening to the car? It was almost as if…no, he couldn't even voice the thought in his head. It was too crazy. "Car's acting up. Probably should get it checked in the next town."

"Should we pull over now? Is it safe to keep driving?" Ben asked.

Eli felt his heart climb into his throat. "Not safe to stop where we are. Nothing I can't handle."

"All right. Murphy out."

The road wound tighter with each passing mile. On Eli's right was nothing but dark, striated canyon rock and Julia's worried eyes. This road was built by detonating explosives. On his left, the rushing water swollen by the spring runoff.

The car sped up, and Eli lifted his foot off the accelerator. Fifty-five miles per hour creeped to sixty. How was this possible when they were climbing uphill, his foot completely off the gas?

Pulling over at this point was not an option. There was little shoulder on either side of the road. Eli pressed his foot into the brake pedal.

Nothing happened.

Eli spoke into his wrist mic. "Ben, next safe place to pull over we need to switch vehicles. We'll change to your car to continue to the safe house and leave Jace behind with this car."

"Got it."

"Why do I have to stay behind? There's a rainstorm coming."

What Eli was tempted to do was verbally rip Jace's head off. The younger agent showed little respect for Eli's command over the situation and almost seemed fine with them being in this precarious position. Protection took sacrifice, and Jace didn't seem up to the task.

"Jace, as soon as we can call out of here, we'll send someone for you. It's not like I'm asking you to stand outside in the pouring rain or leaving you stranded without a car."

The vehicle's speed crept up to seventy miles per hour. A hairpin turn was coming up on the left. Eli continued to tap on the brakes, and the car refused to respond to any command he attempted to get it back under his control.

Do I throw the emergency brake? Will that immediately roll us over the guardrail and into the river?

He yanked the wheel hard left to make the turn. Both Julia and Jace were thrown into their doors.

"Eli…" Julia's voice—not commanding in nature, but riddled with fear. It was his job to protect her, and so far in his care his record was abysmal.

"We're all right. It's going to be fine."

Even his words couldn't convince his heart to stop skipping beats. His head felt tight from the rush of blood pounding at his temples. His fingers ached from his grip on the steering wheel.

Eighty-five miles per hour—the speedometer needle quivered—flirting with ninety miles per hour. Eli rammed his foot into the brake pedal, pumped it several times to get it to engage.

Julia was silent, her hands pressed together and settled at her lips. In the rearview mirror, Ben and

Will's car had drifted far enough back that he no longer had sight of them.

"Ben!"

"I'm here, Eli. We're having trouble keeping up with you. You've got to slow that vehicle down."

"I know! I'm trying!"

Julia gripped the handrail at her head. Jace looked like a wide-eyed child who'd just been put on a roller coaster he didn't want to ride.

Another turn up ahead. At this speed, he wasn't going to make it. "Tighten your seat belts," Eli ordered.

The road hairpin turned again, and Eli gripped the wheel to ease them into the curve long before they had to make it, but the wheel was locked in a straight position. He yanked one side of the steering wheel, but it was as if someone had poured superglue into the mechanism.

There was a brief flash of the guardrail before the bumper pounded into it, the front end of the SUV caved inward. Eli grabbed Julia's hand. The back end of the SUV flipped up, pushing bile up his throat. A loud pop, like gunfire, filled the car, and Eli felt his face smash into the inflated air bag.

And then…blackness.

The air bag deployed into Julia's face, and acrid smoke filled the interior compartment of the vehicle. Julia felt herself somersault forward, the seat belt cutting into her flesh from the force of the hit and subsequent launch into the air. She gritted her teeth against the nausea that built in her gut.

The car screamed as metal tore from metal. Wind howled through the broken windshield. Then came the stomach-lurching drop into the rushing water. Julia shoved her hands into the air bag to brace herself against the dashboard. The SUV met the river, and a shock wave of pain tore through Julia's spinal cord. Water surged around the windows. The vehicle rocked and moaned as it was tossed like a miniature toy in the current.

The worst-case scenario.

Julia patted herself checking for injures. She wiggled her fingers and toes and found them responsive. She glanced to her left. Eli was slumped onto the steering wheel. Even though she feared a possible neck injury—she had to determine if he was breathing. With both hands she leaned over and eased him back—trying to keep his neck midline with a firm hand on his jaw and one clasped behind his neck. A stream of blood flowed down the right side of his face.

"Eli!" She pressed her fingers into the bony part of his jaw, hoping the pain would jolt his consciousness like a defibrillator to an aberrant heart rhythm. Whatever caused the laceration to his forehead had likely knocked him out. Water seeped through the floorboards. A shiver overtook Julia—the frigid water would rapidly drop her body temperature. She struggled to get her cheek as close as she could to Eli's face, stymied by the seat belt, and waited…endless seconds to feel some sort of life against hers.

A warm breath danced across her chilled flesh.

Good—just unconscious.

That was only a momentary reprieve, considering they were bobbing in a wrecked car down an ice-cold mountain river.

She turned around. Jace had his hands pressed into the seat beside him. He was tight, stiff, his eyes wide with fright.

"Jace."

He didn't respond.

"Jace!" Julia yelled.

He blinked…shook his head briefly and then glanced furtively around. "Julia?"

A question, like what a child would pose to a mother when danger was imminent.

Julia released Eli's seat belt and then her own. She stretched her body over Eli's and hit the electric control for his window, holding the button down until the window was level. Icy spring runoff lapped in, sloshing waves drenching Eli's clothes. He still didn't move.

"Jace, we have to get out of this car. Get your seat belt off and roll your window down."

His eyes glazed over. Shock presented itself in many forms. A patient didn't have to hemorrhage to begin the death spiral. It could genesis from a traumatic event that proved too much for the mind to process.

Like impending death.

We're not dead yet.

"Jace! Move!"

Finally, his fingers clumsily reached for his seat belt, and he eased it from his body. Just as he powered his window down, Julia mimicked the same action with her own. "Jace, I need your help with Eli."

His body shook and his teeth started to chatter. "Julia... I can't swim."

Julia closed her eyes. Her hand gripped the fabric of Eli's sport coat. Why was it that medical professionals always *did* end up in the worst-case scenario? The water inside the car was up to her calves and filling faster with the windows open. She inhaled deeply and held her breath for a few seconds to ease the anxiety that raced through her veins. With every beat of her heart, she could feel the dangerously cold blood getting closer to her core.

She opened her eyes and glanced around. As the car rocked down the river, at times it slowed near shallow eddies—Jace would have to jump from the car and try to reach the shore.

"Jace, listen to me. You're not going to have to swim, but I need you to do what I say, when I say it and as quickly as you can do it. Got it?"

He nodded.

"Sit on your windowsill with your feet outside the car, but hold on to the inside strap to keep yourself steady."

Hard reluctance swept over his face.

"Now. Do it right now!" Julia screamed.

He moved quickly and got himself positioned at the window. The water was up to her waist inside the car. Still Eli didn't move.

"When I tell you to jump, you have to jump. Don't think about it."

"But I can't swim."

"The water will be calmer and not deep enough that you'll have to." She could see a turn in the river. Jace's side of the car positioned closer to an area where the surface of the water showed gentle ripples. She hoped it wouldn't be too deep, otherwise she would be asking Jace to leap to his death.

"Doggy-paddle and pull yourself to the bank."

"I can't."

"Jace, please. You have to. I can't get both you and Eli out of this car by myself. Eli can't help himself right now. You can. You've got this. I promise you—it's going to be okay."

His spine straightened with her affirmative words.

"Ready?"

He nodded—his muscles tightened to pounce.

"Push off the car to help you get closer to the shore."

His body tensed. The car's forward progress paused.

"Jump!"

Jace leaped away from the car and gained more distance to the shore than Julia thought possible, his muscles fueled by the primal drive for survival. He landed with both feet in knee-high water. The car swung around and Jace disappeared from Julia's view.

Now what to do about Eli?

The SUV's speed in the water picked up. Julia's side faced downriver. A boulder popped into view, bigger than the size of their vehicle that divided the river in half. There wasn't any way to avoid the collision. What Julia hoped would be a gentle tap instead threw her violently against the side of her door. The force of the river pinned the vehicle momentarily against the rock, and water rushed in through the windows and forced her under.

Julia kicked hard and broke the surface, gasping for air. The water in the car lapped at Eli's chin, and his head dropped forward, dipping his nose into the muddy deluge.

If anything was going to wake him up, it was a face full of snowmelt—still nothing. If he was still breathing then he was pulling the water into his lungs and he would drown. Julia reached out and forced his chin up.

The river now raced through their vehicle. The boulder blocked Julia's exit from the passenger window. The only egress was out Eli's window, swimming against the mighty influx of water.

Julia's body was numb. The only thing she was physically cognizant of was her heart thudding in her chest. There wasn't a way—any way she could see them both surviving. She glanced at Eli. Her arm ached and throbbed from holding his head up.

Do I leave him? Make it out on my own and then pray that help makes it in time to resuscitate him?

She clutched a fist to her chest. In her heart, she knew leaving him would kill him. Could she live with that?

The car shuddered. Their position shifted.

Julia couldn't live with the guilt of not trying everything within her power to get Eli out. Whatever fate God forged for her, it was tightly linked with Eli's. If she lived—then so would he. If he died—she would die trying to save him.

The back end of the car began to rotate. If the water tore the crushed SUV away from the boulder, Julia envisioned being able to pull Eli out the passenger-side window and escape before the icy waters buried them.

Lord, I trust You to help me. I can't save us like this. Please, move this car. Set us free. Give me the strength...

The car dislodged and turned one hundred and

eighty degrees. Julia took a final gulp of air and in one swift movement grabbed Eli under his arms and clasped her arms around his chest. With one hand she reached up and pinched his nose closed. The water helped float his body weight so he rested on top of her but shoved them up against the ceiling. Not a single air pocket remained from which to sneak one more breath of oxygen. Julia reached a hand back and grabbed the top of her window and pulled with all her might, kicking with her feet until they met the bottom edge of the window. Then she shoved with both feet to force their bodies away from the SUV.

Water roared in Julia's ears. Her lungs burned for air. Finally, her face broke through the surface. The torrent ripped Eli from her arms, but he'd surfaced on his back and she slapped at the water and sidestroked to him. After grabbing his arm she looped her arm under his body, her hand on his chin to keep it above the water as his head lolled on her shoulder. Julia positioned their legs downriver and saw another eddy on her right.

Eli was still—perfectly still because he was no longer breathing.

Julia frantically kicked with what remained of her strength until they reached the calmer water. She planted her feet on the bottom of the river and floated Eli to the bank. Then she crawled out of the water and grabbed both of his shoulders and dragged him out.

She nearly collapsed onto his chest as she positioned her cheek over his mouth and lifted his chin to check his breathing, praying he didn't have a neck injury. Nothing. At some point he'd inhaled enough water to cut off his air supply. The faint blue tinge around his lips verified what her heart wanted to deny.

Even though CPR now dictated chest compressions first—she felt that a few breaths might be enough and she didn't know if she had the strength to push as hard and fast as she needed to.

If she gave him one breath—would that be all that he'd need to come back to her?

Dizzy from exertion, Julia took a deep breath and sealed cold flesh with her lips. She exhaled as hard as she could and barely saw a lift in his chest. Again, she repeated what she'd done the first time with only slight improvement in getting more air into his lungs.

Reaching her fingers to his neck, she felt for his pulse. Ten seconds lapsed without a response from his heart.

Now she didn't have a choice.

Julia settled on her knees, right next to his body, clasped her hands together and started chest compressions.

"Eli Cayne…you better breathe! You can't do this to me. Not when…"

What was she about to say? Julia counted to thirty and bent back over him. Pulling his mouth open, again she tried to breathe life into a body that groped for the grave.

Better chest rise this time.

Again, Julia pushed harder on his chest as tears coursed down her face. She was tempted to throw her fist to the sky at God for putting her in this position. Exhaustion would overtake her quickly and she'd be useless.

"Eli!"

A shudder from his body caused her to stop compressions. Murky river water spewed from his mouth and he coughed violently. Julia reached across his body and grabbed his shoulder and hip and rolled him toward her, collapsing on the ground next to him.

Her hand trembled as she laid it on his cheek. She could see the rhythmic rise and fall of his chest and she smoothed her thumb over the doughy coolness of his cheek.

"Eli…open your eyes…please…"

A faint flicker of his eyelashes and finally she could glimpse the pale blueness of his eyes. Unfocused. She could see his pupils weren't dilated. Good. He coughed more and closed his eyes. He became still again, though continued breathing. She examined the cut to his forehead—just a small trickle of watery blood from the gaping wound. At least the icy water had constricted the open blood vessels and stopped any bleeding.

As the last bit of strength seeped from her,

she begged him. "Eli, please, open your eyes. Wake up."

And he did as she asked. His eyes locked on to hers with a flicker of recognition. In that moment, she knew he would live.

His hand found its way to her face. "There are those brown eyes I've been waiting to see."

Again, that phrase that always brought so much peace.

What did it mean?

Julia couldn't hold her eyes open any longer and she slumped onto the riverbank.

SEVEN

Instead of finding herself in the sweet blackness of sleep, Julia stood in the foyer of her old Craftsman bungalow and reeled with confusion. How was she here in her old home? The house was exactly as she last remembered it, including its peaceful calm.

Am I dreaming? Did I die? Is this a memory?

The home had been a gift from her parents. Together they had worked for two years to bring its stories back to life. Hours spent removing layers of dirt and paint to reveal beautiful wooden paneling and heavy rafters. In that time of endless cleaning, sanding and staining, it was the closest she had ever felt to her parents. The months of difficult work showed how much they loved her—not so much in words, but in every moment they spent making her house a home to cherish.

Resting her hand over her heart, Julia listened and could just make out the sound of sandpaper, her father's voice and the lilt of her mother's laughter. Grief overwhelmed her.

Those moments were gone forever. All she had left of them was what she could hold on to from the past. How long would she be able to remember them? Even now the vividness of her memories of them were washed in sepia tones—dull, muted—fading.

A knock at her front door refocused her attention. She glanced at her clothes. The nursing scrubs that she'd been wearing that day.

Today was *that* day.

No, no...no!

Dread bloomed in her chest like a drop of blood in water. Behind that door loomed the monster that would try to steal her life from her. Julia tried to flee from the terror, her feet slipping as she raced backward, but with every step she took back, the door came closer until the knob thrust into her hand.

"Julia?"

A voice.

"I'm coming."

Julia's mind screamed at every action, but her current will couldn't stop the actions of her past self. Her present mind a prisoner of these events— watching them unfold through barely open fingers as the horror movie played on the screen.

Reaching above the door, she grabbed the decorative, antique brass key and slid it into the lock and released the only barrier between her and death.

A blast of light blinded her, and an intense pounding echoed through her head. She reached her hand up and felt wet sand drip onto her. She could hear the distant rush of swift waters. Her eyes focused, and she saw Eli before her, his eyes closed but lips pink.

Julia rolled onto her back and looked up at the sky where dark gray clouds gathered.

What she had just seen—was it true or something her broken neurons pieced together? A false narrative to fill the void? Had she opened the door to her attacker? Did the stress of nearly drowning open her mind to things forgotten?

Because if what she saw was a true memory—how could she forgive herself?

Her attack. Her parents' subsequent death.

All of it had been her fault.

Julia had let the man into her home.

She was relieved when darkness took her again.

The roar of a train broke through Eli's haze as the ground thundered under his body. His eyes darted open in time to see the behemoth coal train curve along the railroad track on the other side of the canyon. Julia lay on her back next to him, her arm reaching out with the tips of her fingers resting directly under his nose. His body was frozen and achy. Tentative fingers reached up to his pounding head and felt the open wound on his forehead. Julia appeared to be sleeping. Her color was pale, but her cheeks held a hint of blush. He reached for her hand and felt her pulse at her wrist—strong and steady.

How long had they been lying here? He struggled and pulled up the sleeve of his sopping wet shirt and checked the time on his watch. If he remembered correctly, they'd gone off the road at approximately three o'clock.

It was over an hour later.

Emotion overwhelmed him, and he rolled over onto his back, quickly brushing away the tears that brimmed his eyelids. He was supposed to keep her safe. How had she done it? Pulled him from the car?

Jace...where is Jace?

Eli sat up too quickly and his vision washed white. He leaned heavily to one side and braced himself until the feeling passed and his eyesight crystallized. He lifted his head slightly. Was someone calling his name? He looked upriver and saw a figure walking along the shoreline on the opposite side.

Friend or foe? That was always the first question. He placed a protective hand on Julia's shoulder until the figure drew closer.

Jace. Alive and well.

"Are you okay?" Eli yelled.

Jace ran. He held his phone in his hand. "Can't

get a signal, but I was able to reach Ben on our com line." Jace pointed behind Eli, and Eli looked up—all he saw was the slope of canyon behind him. The road wasn't visible from his vantage point.

"Is Julia alive?" Jace yelled.

All Eli could do was nod. If he spoke any words, his voice would crumple with guilt. He gave Jace a thumbs-up sign.

"Rescue is delayed. Another accident somewhere," Jace said.

If Eli blocked out all the other noise, he could hear a melee of voices in the distance.

A delay in rescue was not good. They were at risk of hypothermia. Springtime in the mountains was still known for low temperatures at night. If they were stuck here, they could die from exposure.

He reached for Julia. Time to wake up Sleeping Beauty. "Julia. Can you hear me?"

Her eyes popped open, and she licked at her dry lips.

"Anything broken?" Eli asked.

Her eyes were dim. She blinked several times.

"Julia, do you know where you are?"

She lifted her head up and eased herself into a sitting position. Briefly, she turned away from him. Was she hiding tears?

"Talk to me."

It killed him that she wouldn't look his way.

Her body trembled and if he could have given her a dry, warm jacket he would have taken his off.

"Julia, please. Are you hurt?"

Finally, she looked back at him. She pulled her knees up and crossed her arms in front of them, tucking her chin into the crook of her elbow. "I'm not broken...just cold. So tired."

If he could have touched it, he would have torn it down—this wall that was present between them. There was something she was keeping from him. An injury? Anger at his shortcomings on keeping her safe?

"Pulling you from the river took everything out of me," she confessed.

Eli glanced around. How had she done it? He didn't see anyone that could have assisted her.

He stood on wobbly legs and bent over to steady himself with his hands on his knees until the jelly-like feeling waned. Was it just that his strength was sapped or was it complete and utter relief that Julia was alive?

Denial forced his mind to consider only the first option.

"I guess we're even." He reached forward for Julia's hand.

"I guess so," she said, allowing him to pull her up. She swooned, likely from the same light-headedness he suffered. Without thinking, he reached for her and pulled her into a tight embrace.

Realizing his error, he eased her back and

held her with his hands at her shoulders. "Are you okay?"

"I'd just like to compare our rescues. All you did was call 911. I wrestled you unconscious from a crushed car in the middle of a raging river that, I might add, was freezing cold. Oh, and gave you CPR to get you breathing again."

Whatever it was now, it was not the time for him to question her about his take on her emotional state. She had just disclosed that she was the one to save his life. Without her, his family would be planning his funeral. "Yes. That whole lifeguard past is an added benefit to anyone in witness protection. You know we screen for life-saving skills."

Eli hoped he wouldn't have to even the score.

The relief in her eyes replaced the troubled shadow when she saw Jace standing across the river. "Looks like Jace did okay when I forced him to jump from the car." Her brown eyes engaged Eli's. "Did you know he can't swim?"

Surely, there was something profound he should say to her in light of her actions.

Thank you, Julia. You saved my life—and Jace's life. I don't know how I would have lived without you...how I have been living without you.

He shook the thought from his mind. Already, he'd let his feelings cloud his judgment. It was time to put everything aside and do what he was paid to do—which was keeping her alive, not vice versa.

The voices became louder.

"Watch out below!"

Two heavy red bags fell over the side of the rocky face, unspooling rope until they rested at the bottom a few yards away from where Julia and Eli stood. Then a man with a blue backpack began to rappel down the side. Once his feet made contact with the ground, he turned and waved.

Ben. He grinned at the sorry sight of them.

"Didn't quite stick the landing, did you?" He approached them and swatted the top of Eli's shoulder with his gloved hand. "Good to see you're still standing, partner."

Eli gave Julia a reassuring smile. "Me, too. Though both Jace and I have Julia to thank for that. Jace is across the river."

She huddled herself. "Where did you get all this gear?"

Ben motioned them to sit. "This is my other life. I volunteer with alpine rescue. I called a couple of friends who live close to here to help. Let me check the two of you out. Does anything hurt?"

Eli refused to follow his command. "Just get us out of here. Neither of us broke anything. We're just beaten up and cold."

Ben swung his backpack around and opened the smallest compartment. He pulled out a package that held a wound dressing and closed the distance between he and Eli. "Let me at least take care of that cut. All I need is for you to have some excuse to not be at work for the next couple of days."

"Let Julia. She's the nurse."

It surprised him that he said it so quickly. He glanced Julia's way, and she looked at him with faint surprise.

"Let her rest," Ben insisted.

Eli relented and allowed Ben to apply the dressing. "What's the plan?"

Ben waved at Jace and motioned him to sit down. "There's a bad accident a few miles downriver that's tying up the fire department, but since you all are in one piece and able to walk, we can work to get you out of here and then an ambulance should be available by then."

"Glad to have your help. Definitely want to get out of here before nightfall. We're going to need to rethink our next steps as far as Julia is concerned."

Ben nodded. "There's the litter coming down."

Eli looked up and saw a plastic red basket coming down the side of the rock face, relieved that Ben wasn't requiring him to climb out. He knew he didn't have the strength.

Another man rappelled to the bottom and helped ease the litter to the ground.

Ben motioned to Julia. "You're up first. Will is waiting at the top."

Reluctantly, she walked to the litter. Was it the

ropes that bothered her? She sat inside, and Ben pushed gently on her shoulders so she would lie down. "It won't be the smoothest ride, but it's the only way out of here. My guess is that you'd be too exhausted to climb up the rock face even with assistance."

She bit her lower lip but complied. Her fists clenched at her sides as Ben clicked the buckles to keep her in the contraption as it was raised. After Julia was secured, Ben moved to secure additional ropes to the litter to raise it up the rock face.

It amazed Eli how quickly Ben moved. Clearly, Ben was more than the FBI computer geek Eli had considered him to be. Eli had to give him credit. Ben seemed to have considerable mountaineering skills.

"I'll be going up with you—making sure the litter stays steady," Ben said to Julia.

Eli gripped Ben's arm. "Don't let her fall."

A dogged grin swept Ben's face. "Don't forget, she's my witness, too. I have just as much interest in keeping her safe as you do. Maybe I can do a better job."

Eli wasn't sure if Ben was taking a dig or trying to lighten the situation with some good-natured ribbing.

"Too soon?" Ben asked.

Eli smiled. "A little."

"You'll be next up and then we'll work on getting Jace from across the river."

Ben spoke into a radio, and the basket lifted off the ground. Panic twisted Julia's face. Eli could see in her eyes she didn't want to be confined—particularly with a bunch of ropes. He gripped her lower leg as she began to ascend. "I promise you're safe with Ben. I'll see you at the top."

She nodded but didn't seem convinced.

EIGHT

The motion of the litter lurching along the cliff face caused Julia's stomach to roll with nausea. Before they started their drive into the mountains, they had eaten lunch, but the energy she expended to get the three of them out of the SUV had used up every last calorie. She had been starving until the wind started knocking the basket into the canyon wall.

Ben placed a reassuring hand on her forearm. She began to shiver uncontrollably.

How is it possible to be so cold...so tired?

Her body begged for sleep. When would that be possible? What was the next step?

The litter pummeled against the rock. Bits of stone showered her body. Ben removed his hand and gripped the side of the litter and planted his feet against the rock, which further steadied the motion. Julia nervously brushed the pebbles from her face.

"What happened on the road?" Ben asked.

She practiced this tactic every ER shift. Get patients to talk about anything to serve as a distraction from the emotional trauma they were experiencing. Did knowing the tactic make it any less effective?

The litter swayed and tilted Julia's head higher than her feet. She grabbed the sides of the basket.

"You're not going to fall. I promise."

Julia closed her eyes and took a few deep breaths.

Just trust him. He knows what he's doing.

"I don't know," she said. "Eli couldn't control the vehicle. Nothing he did worked. He couldn't even turn the wheel."

"Like someone else was driving?"

Another jerk. Julia tried to calm her shaking. "Yes."

"The SUV could have been remotely controlled."

Julia's heart sank further. "How?"

"All that's required is a laptop. The person doesn't even have to be close."

If that was true...how could she be safe...ever?

"How can we find out for sure?" Julia asked.

"If your car was remotely controlled by someone else, it would be one of the first known cases for the make and model of the SUV you were driving. It's been demonstrated that vehicles can be hacked into. One well-known carmaker recently had a recall for this very thing. We can search for signals to trace, and try to search the vehicle." Ben glanced over his shoulder and grinned. "Might be difficult with where Eli parked it. Hang on…we're almost there."

Hands grabbed Julia and lifted the litter over the edge of the rock face. They set her down by an awaiting ambulance. The team released her and helped her stand up, offering her a blanket and a bottle of water. They assisted her to the ambulance gurney and she sat down—feeling better with a few small comforts. The blanket wrapped her with relief.

Ben kneeled down next to her. His black hair plastered to the top of his forehead, but his green eyes held her with determination. "It's amazing what you did, Julia. I never thought I'd see the three of you alive again. Thank you."

"For what?"

"For sparing me from having to tell all your families that you were gone. That's…the hardest thing anyone has to do. Something tells me you know what I'm talking about."

Julia bit into her lip. She wanted to be strong, but her mind reeled back to one of the many times she had sat with a family as a physician or chaplain delivered devastating news. A child—maybe five or six—hearing that she had been the only survivor of a house fire. That her father had died trying to rescue her younger siblings from the hot, all-consuming flames.

And then Julia's own parents when she learned

of their deaths months after they had been buried. When she grasped what had happened and was physically able to visit their graves, her grandfather was the only thing that held her upright when she nearly collapsed.

"You're a survivor, Julia. This is nothing compared to what you've already been through. Will is going to wait with you. I'm going back down to help get Eli and Jace up."

She nodded but couldn't speak.

Ben turned and left. Would she, though? Be fine? Considering Ben had suggested it was probable the car was remotely controlled by someone?

Eli and Julia sat knee to knee—both on their own ambulance gurney—huddled in blankets and drinking water. Eli thought he'd never want anything to do with water again, but every cell in his body cried out for hydration and he found himself guzzling through three bottles.

"Can I have that?" Eli asked Ben after spotting the water bottle he was holding.

"I already started drinking out of it," Ben said.

"I don't mind." Eli reached his hand out.

Ben surrendered the bottle. "Fine. You can drink it on your way to the hospital."

"I'm not going to the hospital," Eli said.

From the look on Julia's face, he could tell she was none too pleased with him. It didn't really matter. He had to separate his feelings for Julia, his wanting to please her, from his duty to do his job and keep her safe.

"That's the dumbest decision you could make," Ben interjected, who stood near them. The haunting flashes of white and red lights the only thing that broke the settling darkness. They were still waiting for the alpine rescue team to retrieve Jace.

"Well, you haven't known me that long. I'm sure there will be more."

Julia's searched his face. It was unsettling how she seemed to read his thoughts with a glance of her brown eyes. He forced himself to keep her gaze even though his insides squished like melted jelly. It was as if her eyes could know his every thought without him uttering a word. There hadn't been any other woman that affected him this way.

Finally, she spoke. "Eli, you drowned. You died. You have to go to the hospital—"

"It doesn't matter what you tell me. I'm not going." He turned to Ben. "Now we need to re-think exactly where we're going. Until we can figure out—"

Julia stood up, the blanket dropping from her shoulders. "I'm not done talking. I'm the medical professional here, and you're going to listen to what I have to say. You're not out of the woods. The dirty, scummy river water that flooded your lungs could cause infection and fluid to build up, making it hard for you to breathe. You need to be monitored in a hospital setting for at least twenty-four hours."

Eli's heart jumped. The way her eyes implored him, the stern directness of her words, it was more than a nurse concerned for his safety. He put his hands up and motioned her to sit back down. "I get it. I understand what you're saying, but right now it's not going to happen."

"Then we have to think of a compromise," Ben said. "Somewhere you think Julia can be safe but you still get medical attention."

"The ER doctor you met… James. He lives up here—some huge cabin. Let me call him and see if we can stay with him a few days until the two of you get things figured out," Julia suggested.

Eli drank more water as he considered her offer.

"And he can keep his eye on you, which will make me a much more cooperative, compliant witness."

Ben chuckled as if Julia's suggestion was something impossible for her to accomplish.

"Call him," Eli said. Julia wandered away to borrow a cell phone.

Eli knew he could trust only himself and wanted everyone else out of the picture. On the other hand, Julia was right. He was tired. More tired than he dreamed possible. And there was no denying the ache and slight rattle in his chest. What was he risking by not going to the hospital?

Applause drew Eli's attention up the road where

several rescuers were pulling Jace over the edge to safety. They eased him from the litter and handed him the same cursory threadbare blanket and water to drink. Jace looked as wiped as Eli felt. The river had its fun with them and only spat them out because Julia insisted upon it. If he could go his whole life without needing another paramedic, firefighter or ropes expert, it would still be a day too soon.

Julia walked back to the group. "He was home. He says it's fine and they have plenty of room for all of us. They'll be waiting with some home-cooked food to celebrate us being freed from the clutches of death." Julia frowned at their response. "Any humor, people? We're all alive. It's something to celebrate. And ER people always celebrate with food. Have none of you heard about the obligatory chocolate drawer?"

Eli stood from the gurney—the ache spreading through his chest. He coughed several times. "This is the plan, and I'm the senior agent here, so I don't want grief from any of you. Ben, you're going with Jace to the hospital to get him checked out and then you're going home for a good night's rest." He searched for Will, who stood just beyond the reach of the light that drifted from the inner compartment of the ambulance. "Will, you and I are going to take Ben's car to this doctor's house. You can take a quick nap, but then you'll be up keeping an eye on things overnight. One night's rest, and I'll be good to go. We still have a job to do."

Eli looked at Ben, whose mouth gaped open in protest. Eli shook his head to keep Ben silent.

The man refused to heed his warning. "Honestly, Eli, you're in no condition to make any decisions. All three of you need to go to a hospital for evaluation—"

"Julia's friend can look us over. You said yourself we needed a compromise, and this is it." Eli coughed into his hand.

Ben crossed his arms over his chest. "You can't physically protect her right now. I say you and Jace go to the hospital and take a few days off. I'll take Julia to the doctor's house with Will and we'll keep her there until she's rested and we develop another game plan."

Eli pulled Ben away from the group into the periphery just beyond the reach of the rescue lights. He didn't want Julia to hear what he was going to say. He needed Julia to trust him, and so far he hadn't done much to instill that trust in her. Protecting her from the threat on her life was his primary goal, and separating himself from her would only weaken his position of trust in her mind. "I don't want an argument with you. Right now the only one I fully trust is myself—"

"And evidently Will," Ben said.

"I've worked with him longer. This isn't a judgment against you or the job I think you can do. After all, you rescued us. Ultimately, she's my responsibility."

"Eli, you keep convincing yourself you're being professional, but you're not. It's obvious this case is too personal for you and it's affecting your judgment. This is the perfect example."

"Why do you say that?"

"Because you're physically wasted, and you still think you can perform your duties. This choice is putting her at risk."

"It is the best course of action to take."

Ben pressed his lips together and nodded. "Fine. We'll see if she's still alive by morning." He turned on his heel and paced back to the group.

Eli crushed the flimsy water bottle in his fist and threw it to the ground. If Ben was proven right, that Julia died because Eli couldn't defend her in his weakened state, he didn't know if he could ever forgive himself. He needed space and time to think.

Hopefully, this remote location wasn't exactly what the hit man was hoping for.

NINE

While waiting for a response to their knock at the door, Julia could hear a trickle of water moving over smooth river stones at the small creek that wound its way around the fairy tale log cabin. If only that had been the body of water she'd been thrust into.

Laura Solan, Dr. James Solan's wife, opened the door and immediately gathered Julia into a warm hug and in that moment, Julia broke down. Laura squeezed her tighter, smoothing her hand over her dry, crusted hair in an effort to ease her sobs. In that hold was everything that Julia missed from her mother. The sweet, tangy smell of perfume. The quiet, calming, swooshing of Laura's heartbeat in her ear.

"Sweet Julia. What a day you've had." Laura eased Julia back and placed a lightly fisted hand under her chin to lift it up. "You're safe here. We're going to take good care of you."

Laura's tender light green eyes offered the dose

of compassion that Julia needed. Laura brushed her reddish brown bangs from her eyes and offered an open hand to Julia. "Come in. James, they're here!"

Julia felt Eli's hand rest in the middle of her back and edge her into the foyer. His touch lingered far beyond the steps she needed to take, and when he withdrew it, it felt as if a small hole opened in her chest.

"I can't thank you enough for taking us in," Julia said.

"If I can say anything, it's that this tragedy happened at a good time. I'm off for several days and there's nothing I'd like to do more than to take care of you and your friends."

The three of them were standing in the magnificent entryway when Dr. James Solan walked toward them. Julia's eyes were drawn to the three-level open foyer with windows that held a magnificent view of the mountains. The Solans' home was situated in a valley surrounded by the tall granite peaks Colorado was known for.

"Julia, I'm happy to see you again so soon, but not under these circumstances." He reached his hand out and shook Eli's hand. "Why don't you and I—"

Eli coughed into his hand, and Julia's nursing intuition threw up a red flag.

"This is Agent Will Sullivan," Eli said.

James shook his hand, as well. "Will, it doesn't

look like you need to freshen up, so I'll put you in the kitchen with some fresh coffee."

"Is there a couch I could crash on for a few hours?" Will asked. "I'll be our night watchman."

"Absolutely," James said. "I'll show you to a quiet spot and then, Eli—you're with me. Looks like your head needs a few stitches. After that a hot shower and dry clothes. You look to be around the size of one of our two sons, and we've got some boxes with his old clothes that we never got around to donating. Won't be perfect, but at least something better than what you're wearing."

"And you're with me," Laura said to Julia. "In the master bath. Big Jacuzzi tub waiting for you and then a nice hot meal."

Her generosity brought more tears to Julia's face, and she allowed Laura to take her like a child anywhere Laura wanted her to go.

Up the curved staircase and into a master bedroom that filled half the top level. A two-sided fireplace was situated between the master bedroom and the bathroom, and Laura had turned it on to warm the bathroom.

Laura motioned to the things that she had set aside for her. A lush navy blue towel. Several options of body washes and shampoos. She laughed to herself. "A girl can never have too many choices, right?"

Julia smiled. She'd met Laura on a few occasions during parties that the emergency medicine doctors would host at Christmas. Laura was the epitome of a soft place to land. Julia yanked a tissue from a nearby box and covered her eyes.

What a mess I am! The first ounce of kindness that someone shows me and I'm ready to fall to pieces. I'm an ER nurse. I'm used to handling a crisis without being so emotional. What's wrong with me?

Laura motioned to have her sit with her on the side of the tub, and she wrapped an arm around her shoulder. "Julia, do you need to talk?"

At first, all she could do was cry. How could she explain what she felt? Was this what her life was going to be like from now on? Never being able to have a place she could call home again? Was the existence she'd had before, depending only on herself and living completely isolated from everyone except her grandfather, really living?

"Things are such a mess," Julia said.

Laura rubbed her shoulder. "If even half of what James told me has happened, then you have every reason to be crying your eyes out. Has someone really put a hit out on your life?"

"I can't help but believe it's true because ever since I was taken into protective custody, all these strange events have been taking place."

"Did you know Eli before this happened?"

Julia tapped her heels against the side of the tub, her feet still wet and sticky from her dunk in the river. How to answer that question? It was clear that Eli had been significantly involved in her past as far as the Hangman's case was concerned. Did it go beyond that? The flashes she began to have seemed like memories cresting the surface of her consciousness. Was Eli the trigger? Or was it just the trauma of what she had lived through that caused her normal defense mechanisms to break down and the events to surface?

"He was the detective on my case after my accident."

"It was hardly an accident. You were almost murdered." Laura sighed. "It's just this look he has in his eye whenever he glances your way. Even in the few moments I saw him with you, I could tell he didn't want you out of his sight."

"He's doing a job. It's nothing more than that."

A coy smiled played on Laura's lips. "Julia, it's so much more than that. It's the same look James gave me when I knew he fell in love with me."

Julia's heart skipped a beat. The word so foreign in her mind when all she'd felt was lost love over the past couple of years. Her parents. Nearly losing her career.

"We can contemplate all that when you're rested." Laura reached behind Julia and turned the water on. "I'm slightly more round and shorter than you are, but this pair of sweats should get you through the night at least. When you come down, leave what you're wearing in here and I'll run it through the wash and have it ready for you by morning. All I want you to do tonight is eat and sleep and not get up at any particular time. Nurse's orders."

Julia smiled. If she was one—she had also better listen to one. Though Laura's specialty had been the neonatal ICU.

"Lotion and a hair dryer are by the sink. New toothbrush and toothpaste, as well. Living up here, you never know who's going to stop in stranded with few if any of their belongings." She stood. "It's been a long time since I've gotten to chat with you. I always felt like you were the kind of girl who could be the daughter I never had, and I know you lost your own mother, so take this with the love it's meant to convey." Laura ran her fingers through the water, testing the temperature, and then adjusted the knobs slightly. "I know things have been hard for you, Julia, but there are people here to help you. You are not going to go through this alone. I won't allow it."

All Julia could offer in response was a tired smile. "I can't thank—"

"Saying thank you is generous and not necessary. James says you're family and you can stay here as long as you need to."

And with those words she left Julia alone.

Julia stood in front of the mirror. Her clothes, now dry, stuck to her in a wrinkled mash of crusty fabric. Her hair was matted with leaves, and branches stuck in the tangles. She reached her arms out, noting the deep purple bruises that dotted areas on her lower forearms. Nothing that wouldn't heal. Nothing that would leave a scar.

At least a physical one.

She brushed her fingers over the scars on her neck, new tears coursing down her cheeks. Would she ever stop crying? The scarf she'd been wearing was long gone. Both of Eli's shoes were claimed by the river. Though the act was generous, the clothes that Laura had left her were not going to cover up what she most wanted to hide. Even when her clothes were washed, these scars would be exposed. People would see. People would ask her. She'd have to share her story.

Would that crush her or save her?

The table was set to evoke peaceful solace. Eli felt almost human. The expected muscle soreness hedged with a hefty dose of ibuprofen. Dr. Solan had numbed up the cut on his forehead, washed it out and closed it with five stitches. He was clean and dressed in dry clothes that fit better than expected. Will, having not had a free rafting trip, remained in his business suit and sat next to Eli. Julia sat across from him in a loose-fitting pair of sweats.

Would she ever drop her hand from her throat?

The smell of bacon and earthy corn from Laura's chowder caused Eli's stomach to turn over with anticipation. Even the fresh, cold water was taking the edges off his exhaustion.

James sat at the head of the table. "Shall we say grace?"

Julia dutifully dropped her head. Eli looked down, his hands settled in his lap. These moments felt strange to him. He longed for connectedness—this type of connectedness. Friends and family sharing a meal together. He had family, but they were distant. Rarely did they communicate unless there was an emergency.

"Father, we thank You for keeping Eli and Julia safe today. Bless our time together. Thank You for providing Eli and Will to be watchful protectors over Julia and allow them to bring to justice this criminal who threatens Julia's life. Amen."

Julia repeated the Amen. Eli lifted his eyes. Laura began to scoop full ladles of the soup into their bowls. A basket of homemade white dinner rolls passed by, and Eli hoped taking three wouldn't seem too aggressive. Next was the soft, real butter that he slathered on, followed by cherry jelly.

If only all was perfect.

What Eli couldn't deny was the ceaseless tightness and pain in his chest. Between each bite of chowder he coughed. At one point, he brought a clean white napkin to his lips and hacked into it. Bringing it away, he noticed a slight pink tinge.

Julia glanced his way at just the right moment and saw it, as well.

"James," Julia said, motioning to Eli. "Can you check Eli out? I think he might be getting some fluid buildup in his lungs."

"What?" Eli shook his head in defiance. "Really, I'm fine. Just coughing up some of that extra river water that's camped out. Nothing to worry about." Again, he was racked by a coughing fit.

James stood from the table. "Nonsense. I think Julia's excellent nursing judgment is at play here. Come with me."

Will clambered to his feet. "Eli, seems like a good time to do a perimeter check."

"Good idea." Eli stood, as well. "A terrific meal, Laura. Thanks so much for making us feel so welcome."

James motioned for Julia to follow. "I'll need you, too, Julia—an extra set of medical hands will be nice and Laura tends to freak out about any patient over ten pounds."

Laura rolled her eyes. "And you tend to freak out at anything less than ten pounds, so we're even. Take Eli up to the loft. All your medical gear is up there and it's where I was going to settle Eli and Julia for the night anyway."

Once they crested the staircase, James motioned for him to sit on the couch that sat along the wall. The ceiling, planked with simply stained pine boards, narrowed into a peak. French doors led to a deck that overlooked the gentle brook that looped through their property.

"Really, Dr. Solan. I'm fine." Eli clenched his teeth to keep from coughing, but despite his best efforts more spasms racked his chest.

"When did you start to feel this way?" James asked.

Eli glanced Julia's way—there was that look again. One eye slightly narrowed with a slight smirk to her face. That look was more effective at keeping him truthful than being connected to a lie detector. "Not long after coming out of the water—definitely once we made it out of the canyon."

James pulled an orange trauma pack from the closet, zipped open a small compartment, fished out a small device and placed it on Eli's finger. "Let's see where your oxygen level is at."

Julia sat on a chair across from him. "I don't know how long he wasn't breathing. It took less than a minute of CPR to get bring him back to me."

Eli straightened a little bit at her statement and saw a faint rush of crimson color her cheeks. It was an odd way to phrase what had happened unless she had something beyond just a need for protection from him. Did she have feelings for him? Could she?

James pulled out a stethoscope and looped it around his neck. "Eli, you nearly drowned, and we only say that you nearly drowned because you didn't die. The fluid in your lungs is filling up the tiny air sacks. It's why you're coughing so much." He laid the stethoscope against his chest. "Take a deep breath."

Eli complied. James frowned. The monitor on his finger began to beep.

Julia stood up and looked at the reading. "Eighty-six percent."

James crossed his arms over his chest. "That's not good, Eli. Even at altitude, we'd want you higher than that. Your lungs sound junky—a very official medical term for stuff being there that shouldn't. A hospital is the safest place for you to be."

How could he make them understand? He wouldn't go. "That's not possible. I need to stay here with Julia."

James turned to Julia. "I'm willing to start treating him here if you'll help watch over him, but I can't stay up all night because I have to drive down to work in the morning."

"I'll do what needs to be done unless he gets too sick," Julia said. "But, Eli, if I say you have to go to the hospital, then you can't argue with me."

For her, he was willing to do it. To be sick as long as they weren't separated.

James faced Eli. "I work with volunteer rescue up here, so I have items on hand that will help with this problem. I'll only institute treatment if you promise me that you won't give Julia grief if she says you're too sick to stay here. Deal?"

"Deal."

"Here's the plan. A dose of a diuretic. This will pull the extra fluid from your lungs. I'll let Julia repeat the dose one time if she feels like you need it in six hours. I'm putting you on some oxygen until your levels can be normal on room air."

Julia motioned Eli off the couch to the bed and pulled the covers down and then arranged the multitude of pillows so he could rest with his back against the headboard. "And you'll need to be resting. It will help your breathing if you're sitting upright."

Dr. Solan came up next to him and handed him a small white tablet and set a black bag on the bed that held a green oxygen bottle. Julia took a package from him that contained clear tubing.

"Take this," James said. "It's the medication."

Julia extracted the tubing from the package and after he swallowed the medication placed the prongs in his nose. James turned on the tank and he felt the rush of a cool, swift stream of oxygen fill his nose. He took several deep breaths, which led to more coughing. Julia rested her hand in the middle of his chest—likely from instinct, but then it remained, which caused the soft beeping on the monitor to chirp faster, his physical response to her touch betrayed by a tiny probe at the tip of his finger.

"We'll shut that portion of the monitor off so you can get some rest," James said.

Eli held his hand out to shake the doctor's hand. "This is going above and beyond. I won't forget it."

"No thanks necessary. I'm hoping my good deeds here will convince Julia that she needs to return to the adult ER world."

Julia pulled a chair close to Eli's bedside. "He'll be a good enough dose of adult medicine that I won't feel the need to *ever* go back."

Eli smiled. The best nurses always had a sarcastic sense of humor to help put the patient at ease.

"Remember what I said," James scolded. "If you're not better by morning you're coming down the mountain with me, and your agency will have to send others to keep Julia safe."

James handed Julia his stethoscope. "Listen to those lungs every few hours. If they still sound like they do now and he still needs the oxygen, then repeat the Lasix dose. We'll have a good idea by morning if he's going to fly or not."

Eli saluted the physician on his way out. Which left him and Julia alone.

Julia grabbed the sheet and covered the lower half of his body. "Are you comfortable?"

More coughing. He nodded. Knife-sharp spindles of pain shot like electricity through his chest, and he pressed his arms into his ribs to counteract the pain.

When he leaned forward, she rubbed her palm against his back and briefly her hands wandered into his short lengths of hair where she massaged his neck. Too soon, she withdrew her hand, and he settled back against the pillow.

"Sorry," she said. "Kids are put at ease more quickly with a calming touch, but it probably doesn't translate well to adults."

"I didn't mind." Was it wise for him to say that?

"Well, forgive me if I absentmindedly rustle your hair like I do my younger patients."

This whole scenario confused him. Eli didn't have anything left. No weapon. No credentials. The river had stripped everything from him. He felt about as naked as a man could feel. Even his own clothes were unworthy to be worn.

Was that how Christ felt? On more an intellectual level, Eli had been intrigued by Jesus' story. The claims of Christianity were outrageous. God becoming man as a sacrifice to save mankind. Christ, too, had been stripped of everything when he came to earth.

Imagine leaving heaven and landing here. Even what we think of as majestic mountains must have seemed like the most impoverished shantytowns compared to the grandeur He normally dwelt.

From a pure common sense point of view, God creating the world made the most sense to Eli. Without outside intervention...everything fell apart. What he knew he missed with God was the emotional connection. It was what Julia had. What he was jealous of.

What he was beginning to feel that he could have—that he absolutely needed—with Julia.

And now their roles were reversed. It wasn't that Eli felt on the verge of death—just physically exhausted, but nothing that a good night's sleep couldn't fix. But how well could he protect Julia at this moment in time? He'd have to depend on Will's good judgment to get them through the night. How had Will scored on his last weapons test?

Regardless of how Eli felt, he'd have to allow Julia to take care of him if he ever hoped to recover quickly enough to do the job he needed to do.

Eli both loved and hated the idea.

Julia closed her eyes and eased her head back. Usually, it was easy for her to slide into her role as a nurse. Providing medical care for Eli wasn't the problem. Being physically close to him would be the hard part.

He's going to pick up on this. He's going to get a sense that I'm attracted to him. That I want to know about our past together.

Before the thoughts could take over her rational mind, she stood from the chair and placed the stethoscope in her ears.

"I need to listen to your lungs." She lifted the

top of his T-shirt and snaked the end of the stethoscope under it to his left chest. "Take a deep breath." He complied, and she kept her fingers firmly on the bell so her fingertips didn't brush against his skin, fearing her touch would give away her stammering heartbeat. She repeated the same thing on the right side. With her left hand, she reached for his upper arm, her hand settling over the concave curve of his biceps as she eased him back up to a sitting position. She lifted the bottom of his shirt and listened to his lungs again and then quickly pulled the shirt back down.

"How do I sound?" Eli asked.

"Junky."

"Dr. Solan made that word up. That can't be a medical term."

Julia smiled. "If you said that phrase to any medical person across the country, they would know exactly what you were talking about. That means *it is* an official medical term."

The oxygen tank lay next to him on the other side of the bed and she leaned over Eli to check the amount James had placed him on. One liter. She checked his oxygen level on the finger probe. It still hovered around 89 percent. Not terrible for altitude, but might as well get him to a more normal level, since they were giving the oxygen. She turned the dial until it read two liters.

As she was about to straighten up, she felt Eli brush his fingers, warm and tender, across her cheek and tuck her hair behind her ear. As she stood, he reached for her and held her hand.

"Julia…"

Every quirky cartoon she'd watched as a child rushed into her mind, and it wouldn't have surprised her if Eli could see her heart bounding from her chest, little pink hearts fluttering out of her eyes.

He tugged at her hand and drew her closer, bringing one hand up and resting it behind her neck, stroking her hair between his fingers. The strength in her knees withered, and she steadied herself with a hand on his shoulder as he continued to ease her closer.

Ever so slowly, she inched toward him. He guided her face next to his and rustled his cheek against hers, soft, musky and freshly shaven— her resolve to pull away disappeared. His touch contained so many things missing from her life.

Safety. Protection. Love?

Both of his hands caressed her neck, and it was the first time that kind of touch didn't cause the unwanted onset of a panic attack. He eased her back slightly and then pressed his lips against hers.

Soft. Warm. Gentle. Searching.

Everything she expected from a first kiss.

Julia leaned in just a little, and—

A quick three knocks rapped on the door. Julia pulled away from Eli and managed to settle herself back into her chair before Will came through the door.

"How's the patient?" he asked.

Julia cleared her throat. "We're good. I mean—"

"Julia's taking great care of me," Eli said. "How are things downstairs?"

Will's eyes roved between the two of them.

Had he picked up on their too-brief kiss?

"Fine," he said. "I contacted Quentin and gave him a heads-up as to what's going on. Jace was checked but released from the hospital. Ben took him home. In the morning, we all need to get back to the office by noon. Quentin says he's got some information that could move the case forward. Then we'll decide what the next best option is. Considering our state and that this cabin is off the treaded path—he's fine with us being here for one night. He doesn't want to put this family at risk beyond that."

"Great. Thanks for the update, Will."

He bowed out and closed the door behind him.

Eli reached for Julia's hand again.

"I'm sorry. I shouldn't have done that."

An ache settled at the base of Eli's throat. It wasn't the first words he imagined he would say after a kiss—their first kiss. Death would have been better than him living through the look in Julia's eyes.

When she came near, something overcame him.

Something unexpected. Something he'd never felt for another woman before. His heart cried out to somehow adequately thank her for saving his life. Words were never Eli's gift, and yet the physical expression of his emotional connection to her couldn't have come at a worse time.

He had a job to do and he couldn't fail at it. An emotional connection, especially acting on it, would jeopardize them both. It already had done so, and even though Julia had pulled him from the river that nearly took his life—the feelings he had for her would do the same if he didn't figure out a way to control them.

Eli wished he'd drowned, because his ineptitude at being able to verbally express these feelings reflected a pain in Julia's eyes that he didn't want to inflict.

He'd hurt her...deeply.

"I mean, I'm sorry but I'm not sorry..." He exhaled and the pain in his chest flared. "There are so many things wrong with what I just did. It's completely unprofessional and..."

Julia brushed a tear from her eye and offered him a weak smile. "I get it. I really do. It's been a trying day for everyone. We just need to get some sleep."

What he never wanted to do, he'd done in spades...caused her more pain. How could he make this right? If he didn't fix it, Quentin would pick up on what was happening and assign another agent to her. Eli couldn't let that happen.

"It's not the right time," he said. Would there ever be a good time?

She stood from the chair and crossed to the couch, lying down and pulling an afghan over her. Even in her mildly disheveled state, she looked beautiful. Her normally curly blond hair soft and blown straight still tousled from his touch. Was there an opportunity for them to get past this? Would it ever be possible to have normal lives together?

"You're him, aren't you?"

Eli blinked quickly. "Who?"

Julia tucked the blue-and-green afghan under her chin, her scars hidden—the piece of knitted love a better protector for her than he was. "When I finally came out of the fog of my brain injury, my grandfather told me that my parents had died on the way to the hospital to see me."

Eli clutched his sheet in his hands. On the surface, she was trying to be brave—to act as if she had weathered and overcome the horrid events of her life. But in those dark eyes a relentless storm brewed.

"Going to my parents' graves was the hardest thing. Seeing their names in stone. Never getting to say goodbye." She rolled on her back and stared and the ceiling. "My father and I were very close. Daddy's girl was an understatement. When he was gone, I didn't feel like anyone could make me feel as safe as he did."

Where was this going? Any proffered sentiment he tried would seem underwhelming.

"My grandfather said there was a man watching over me. That the nurses told him a police officer would come and visit me early in the morning every day."

"I was waiting for a witness to wake up. I had a serial killer on the loose."

"He also said there was a police officer matching the description the nurses gave him at my parents' funeral, but they never spoke."

"I was there in hopes of finding the killer— to see if he liked to watch the fallout of what he had done."

"And that this policeman helped with my physical therapy so my grandfather wouldn't have to pay for extra sessions."

What could Eli say to that? She was exposing his interest in her in quite a methodical manner. She could put the best interrogators to shame with her skill in questioning.

She brushed more tears from her eyes. "That man... That was you..." She looked at him, but he turned away.

He wasn't strong enough to take it.

"You've made me feel like it's possible for another man to make me feel safe. It was a true gift

and I just wanted you to hear it from me, since…
evidently…we can't be together."

He wanted to convince her otherwise—his
mind screamed at him to talk her away from this
cliff she was about to go over. She was walling
herself off from him—that was what this was.
His professional training demanded he stay silent. This was better for them both in the end. He
could complete his professional duties emotionally unattached and keep her alive.

That was what was most important.

TEN

The night provided the rest Eli needed. He couldn't believe how much better he felt. There was the muscle soreness, bumps and scrapes induced by the car wreck, but his breathing was unencumbered and he'd successfully been weaned off the oxygen. Even the coughing was infrequent.

Julia woke him once in the night that he remembered, though he knew she checked on him frequently. She listened to his chest again and he kept his hands firmly underneath the covers. After that, she removed the oxygen from his nose and sat next to his side for a good twenty minutes until she seemed satisfied that his oxygen level would stay normal.

They'd exchanged only the necessary words. It frustrated Eli that she was so business-as-necessary, but he was responsible for this distance between them. Now he had to live with it—even if it was the last thing he wanted to do. It was the necessary thing.

After Laura served them a fresh batch of cinnamon rolls, bacon and coffee, Eli felt as if running a marathon was within reach. A couple of ibuprofen and he would be good to go.

No events overnight. Even Julia gave the appearance of feeling rested, though he guessed from the slowness of her movements that the same aches and pains bothered her.

Time to catch this killer.

The car was quiet as they drove out of the mountains. Julia seemed enraptured by the scenery. Will dozed in the backseat. Once they got back into the Denver metro area, Eli dropped Will off and swung by his place for a fresh business suit. Julia fell asleep on his couch as he showered, evidently more exhausted from nursing him overnight than she let on.

Once changed, he searched through his dusty books until he found what he was looking for. He pulled it from the cardboard box and walked into his living room, where Julia was now awake and watching television.

He offered her the Bible. "I know it's not an adequate replacement for the one you lost—I mean you lost a lot of personal things in the river, but it's new and I know the person who gave it to me would want you to have it."

Julia reached up with tentative fingers and took it from him. She peeled open the black leather cover and read the inscription. "For the man who watched over Julia. Know that there is one who watches over you. Hank Galloway." Julia inhaled swiftly. "My grandfather. He gave this to you?"

Eli cleared his throat. "The nursing staff sent it to the police department with a note. They said Hank waited for a few days around the clock at the rehab center hoping to catch me, but I never returned."

"Why didn't you come back?"

He swallowed hard. The truth—once it was clear that she was healed from her brain injury, he'd wanted to get to know her better and his initial goal in helping her recover from her injuries to aid him in catching a killer had morphed into something more, but Eli knew personal involvement with Julia could threaten the case and they had nabbed their killer. He had run out of excuses to visit her and he wouldn't risk letting this criminal go free because a jury questioned whether or not his involvement with the only surviving victim clouded his investigation. Best to stay away.

"Your case was solved and your testimony..."

"Wouldn't have been helpful with my brain damage?" Bitterness etched her voice.

She closed the cover and tapped her fingers on the surface. Something brewed—something she wanted to say. Her dark eyes held his. "Thank you. This means a lot to me."

Eli picked up his keys. "Let's get moving. Time for you to meet Quentin."

The distance to the marshals' office was short compared to the drive they'd already covered. As Eli roved through the cubicles, a few agents playfully elbowed him in the gut.

"Cayne, what—you have to fake your own death to get a kiss from a beautiful girl?"

"It's the only way a good-looking girl *would* kiss him."

A surge of heat flushed Eli's face, and Julia looked as if she wanted to crawl under a rock.

Eli waved them off. "At least I *can* get someone to save my life. You two, on the other hand, better hope for some blind rescuers if looks come into play."

They laughed, and Eli motioned Julia forward. He ushered her into Quentin's office and pulled out a chair for her.

"Eli." Quentin reached out. "Good to see you're in one piece."

Ben rapped on the door and entered the office, as well.

Ben shook Eli's hand. "Seriously, you look like a new man. Who would have guessed you could look so good when you were a dead, drowned rat just yesterday?"

Eli shrugged. "I have Julia and Dr. Solan to thank. They brought me back to good health. Now that we have our heads above water, we need to get control of this case. What do you have?"

"First things first," Quentin said, offering his

hand to Julia. "Julia, I'm Quentin Archer. I don't know where Eli's manners are—I thought I taught him better than that."

She smiled and shook his hand briefly. "Julia Galloway—nice to meet you."

Quentin straightened and opened the top drawer of his desk. "These are for you. New credentials and a service weapon. Don't lose them. Accounting is angry enough about the car."

Eli pulled them toward him. He felt more like himself. Previously, stripped of everything, but now physically healed and with all the accoutrements of his profession back in his hands. He holstered the weapon and felt whole.

Quentin settled behind his desk. "Let's move forward. Since the safe houses seem to not be working out for us, I've decided to let Julia stay in her own home. We'll provide her two agents overnight to make sure nothing untoward happens again. During the day—" he nodded to Eli "—she'll be in your company until we sort out the details of the hit file."

"Sir, Will mentioned that you had some new information," Eli said.

"Yes. FBI Forensics was able to match the set of prints lifted from the hit package." Quentin rustled through some papers on his desk. "Ryder Dymond. He's got a litany of charges for breaking and entering, shoplifting and selling illegal drugs, but nothing violent."

Ben smirked. "Why do these criminal lowlifes always have weird names?"

Quentin shrugged. "We've had a team casing his house since yesterday. No male presence. A woman and a child live there. The house is rented by Ryder and Harper Dymond, so we're assuming she's his wife. Mr. Dymond hasn't showed his face around the premises. The wife may know something, but we haven't interviewed her yet."

Eli thrust his hands in his pockets. "Sir, I'd like to be more actively involved in investigating this case. If it's true that Evelyn Roush's demise was possibly by the hand of some unidentified partner of the Hangman, then I think we need to go back. Look at all the victims in his series again. Did you get me approval from the Justice Department to interview Heller?"

"Still waiting to hear back," Quentin said. "I don't see anything wrong with reexamining the original case, but you'll need the cooperation of Aurora police."

"Don't worry—I've got connections there. Also, I'd like to interview Ryder's wife," Eli said.

Quentin smoothed his hands together. "Yes, I think it's a good time to see if we can shake something out of her. I don't think Mr. Dymond will be showing his face there any time soon. The wife seems pretty innocuous."

"It's settled, then." Eli turned to Ben. "Can you

take Julia back to her house and hang with her until the night crew gets there?"

"I want to go with you," Julia said. She'd been so quiet—Eli had forgotten to try and shield her from the conversation.

Quentin placed his elbows on his desk. "Julia, you're a protected witness, and we need to do a better job of ensuring your safety. It's outside just about every protocol I can think of to have you go with Eli. Your home is the safest place for you to be."

"Except he knows where I live," Julia pressed.

"I understand, but with our presence nothing will happen to you there," Quentin assured her.

"But you can't guarantee that—you haven't been able to yet."

"Julia—" Quentin started.

"I can help. I think...no, I know that I'm remembering things."

Eli nearly fell over. "What?"

"I'm getting flashes. I think they're memories."

"Why didn't you say—"

Julia cut him off with a quick glance.

Eli took a deep breath in and held it. It was his fault. When had he given her the opportunity to share this? Truth was last night he'd cut her off at the knees.

"What have you remembered?" Quentin asked.

"Pieces from that day. Getting ready for work.

Going to the door. Opening it…" Julia's voice trailed. Her head bent down.

Open. That was the key word. If she willingly approached the door then…

"Did you recognize your attacker?" Eli asked.

"What I think is that I willingly let the person in. The first time I remembered something, he was inside my house, but I didn't know how he got there. I haven't been able to see the person—he's all fuzzy. The next time, I remembered hearing the person call my name and unlocking the door. It ends there."

"Julia, that doesn't help us," Ben said. "Quentin's right. It's safer for you to be secured. There are too many other variables when you're out and about."

"You're wrong." Julia glared at Eli. "Being around people who are part of the case can trigger more of these memories. I don't think it's outside the realm of possibilities that I could identify the man who attacked me. I honestly don't think it was Dr. Heller."

Ben blew his hair from his eyes. "Quentin," he implored. "We absolutely cannot let her do this. Do you know how foolish we look? First, the carbon monoxide poisoning and then she nearly drowns in a river. If you allow this, it's asking for more trouble."

A torrent of thoughts rushed through Eli's mind. What he knew was he felt more in control of the situation when they were together. Perhaps she was right. Julia could be the linchpin that could break the case wide-open.

"I'm okay with it," Eli said. "It's not a perfect scenario, but Julia's right. She's been attacked at her house. Keeping her there twenty-four-seven could just make her an easier target. If she's roving with us, it makes it more difficult to pin her down."

Quentin drummed his fingers. "I'm willing to go along with it but, Eli, if this goes south in any fashion, then your job and my job are both on the line. We're off standard operating procedure. That would be cause enough for termination. Any more near misses and you can kiss your career in law enforcement goodbye."

"Understood, sir."

Ben threw his hands up. "I can't believe the two of you. No wonder the U.S. Marshals' office is such a disaster. Your agents are leaving because you're asking them to risk their lives unnecessarily. Quentin, I'm happy to protect Julia while she's in a secure environment, but this is too risky. I don't want to go on this interview. It's like you're delivering her right to a potential assassin. It's insanity."

Quentin stood. "Fine, Ben. We'll use your assets back at her house. I want everything rechecked. Surveillance equipment. New locks. You and Jace can head that up today. Be sure it's ready by the time Julia is home tonight. Are we good on that?"

"Yes, sir. Absolutely."

Eli rustled his hand through his hair. What little he knew of Ben, it surprised him how adamant he was on this issue. Ben didn't seem like the type to play completely by the book. As an agent— he understood Ben's concerns about the possible loss of his job, but it was just an interview with a woman and her child.

Could these two people be another key in unlocking Julia's memory?

The drive to Ryder Dymond's abode had been quiet…unnervingly quiet for Julia's taste. What did they talk about now? How could they get through these days together…maybe even weeks before ferreting this plot out?

All this tense silence was going to drive Julia crazy.

Eli parked the car on the street. The surveillance team didn't have any new information. The neighborhood was 1980s tract housing. Cookie-cutter homes differentiated only by their faded paint color.

Eli removed his seat belt. "Just stay a couple of steps behind me." He adjusted the mic at his wrist. "If there's trouble, the team is just down the block. You get somewhere safe, and I'll worry about myself."

She did as instructed. Eli rapped on the door and a woman dressed in a dirty floral housecoat came to the screen door. Her hair was a knotted mass of tangles pulled up in a messy bun. A boy, whom Julia figured to be about eight years old, hovered next to her—his brown eyes matched his mother's, though his hair was lighter in color.

"Harper Dymond?" Eli asked.

"Yes?"

Julia could feel the woman's trepidation as if her heartbeat broadcast wirelessly directly to Julia's. It matched what she'd felt just days ago.

"I'm U.S. Marshal Eli Cayne." He held up his credentials for her to study. "I need to ask you a few questions."

Surprisingly, she opened the door. Eli stepped inside and then motioned Julia to follow. Toys cluttered the front living room, and it seemed as if the young boy had the run of the house.

The screen door slammed behind Julia, and each muscle in her body tensed—the sound too similar to the gunshot she'd nearly suffered.

"Thanks for being open to a few questions. This is Julia Galloway—she's…"

"I recognize you from the news coverage from the Hangman's trial," Harper said, shaking Julia's hand with the strength of a timid mouse.

Julia couldn't quite put her finger on it, but there was something about this woman—as if perhaps they'd crossed paths but were never formally introduced. The grocery store? Had she brought her son to the ER for a visit?

"Do you mind if we sit?" Eli asked.

Harper removed the boy's toys from the furniture and motioned for them to sit on a threadbare love seat. Eli perched on the edge, whereas Julia nestled herself in the corner—the hairs on her neck prickled at having to sit right in front of the picture window.

The boy jumped backward onto the couch and seated himself between Julia and Eli. "I'm Miles!"

Julia awkwardly reached out her hand and he shook it with gusto. "It's nice to meet you, Miles. My name's Julia."

"Miles, please…leave the poor woman alone."

"It's okay," Julia said.

"She works with kids," Eli offered. "I don't know if you're aware, Mrs. Dymond, but a package was delivered to Ryder's parole officer. It was a packet of information used in murder-for-hire plot, and it had Ryder's fingerprints on it. Do you know how the parole officer got that package?"

Harper fiddled with the end of her zipper. "I don't."

"Do you happen to know where Ryder might be?" Eli asked. "We'd really like to speak with him and get this whole matter cleared up."

"I don't know where he is." She blew wayward

strands of hair from her eyes. "He's a no-good...
ever since..."

What was it she didn't want to say? Ever since
what?

"You're sure you don't know where he might
be?" Eli pressed.

"Ryder and the things he does when he's not
home have gotten him into more trouble than I
care to know about."

"Mrs. Dymond, is there anywhere you could
think of as to where he might go?"

"He's run off before. Won't tell me nothin'.
Sometimes I get a few dollars in the mail, but it's
never enough to feed this child."

The more Harper talked, the more Julia felt she
knew this woman. She began to study her and the
house more. No photos were visible. Sometimes
people in law enforcement said that was a bad sign
of poor family connections, but Julia thought it
could also be people not wanting to be haunted by
their pasts. The house was cluttered, but not hor-
ribly unclean. If Harper's hair was combed and
she wore pants and a nice shirt with just a hint
of makeup, she'd be a striking woman. Even in
her hoveled appearance Julia's self-esteem plum-
meted.

"Has Miles ever been to the hospital before?"
Julia asked. "Children's Hospital?"

Harper planted her hands between her knees.
The question didn't seem difficult, but Harper

acted as if she were being forced to walk a tight-rope. "Why would you ask that?"

"It's just that you look familiar to me, and I'm wondering if I took care of Miles before."

"Julia's a pediatric ER nurse," Eli clarified.

"You're a nurse?" Miles bounced up and down on the couch's cushions.

Julia tried not to hunch her shoulders too noticeably.

"Once when I was doing my superhero moves—" Miles leaped from the couch and raced around the room holding his arms out like Superman "—I dove off the steps and had to have stitches right here." Miles collided into Julia and pointed to his eyebrow. Just below it was the faint, slightly raised scar from a stitched laceration.

"He didn't go to Children's then," Harper said. "We weren't living here when that accident happened."

"It looks like you were very brave," Julia said to Miles.

Eli cleared his throat. "Harper, any information you could tell us about where Ryder might be would go a long way in keeping you from scrutiny. I wouldn't want anyone to think that you were aiding a fugitive from the law."

Harper's eyes widened. "Is that what he is? A fugitive? Just 'cause he's not around to answer a few questions?"

"It's more than that," Eli said. "Julia's life is at

risk. I don't know if you're aware, another woman has recently been murdered just like the Hangman's other victims, and we don't know if the real killer is on the loose. At this point, it would be difficult for us to say that Ryder is not involved in these crimes, because you won't answer our questions and we can't find him."

Harper dried her palms on her withered dress. "I don't know what to tell you. I'd help if I could… I really would. Our family has had enough tragedy. I just want to move—"

"What kind of tragedy?" The question slipped from Julia before she could help herself. Was it something that brought Harper and Miles into contact with her? A medical crisis at the hospital?

"It's nothin' I want to get into with a stranger, but we've seen our fair share of death. That's all I'm going to say."

Miles tugged at the end of Julia's sleeve. "Do you have any scars you can show me?"

The scars at Julia's neck burned as if they were lit on fire. She adjusted the scarf around her neck to ensure that they remained hidden.

"Miles!" Harper yelled. "That's not a polite thing to ask someone."

"Mrs. Dymond—are you sure you don't know Julia? You've never met her before?" Eli asked.

Harper shook her head. The wall was up, and cold defiance had set in. Eli's shoulders dropped.

He seemed to sense what Julia knew—Harper wasn't going to tell them anything else at this point.

Miles continued to tug at her shirtsleeve, and she turned to face him.

"Miss Julia—did you ever take care of my cousin? The one who died?"

ELEVEN

Eli sat in the car facing Harper's house waiting to back out until Julia had her seat belt secured.

"That was…odd," Julia said.

"I'd have to say that was the quickest I was ever muscled out of a house by someone half my size." Eli backed out of the driveway wondering why Harper refused to talk about the cousin her son had mentioned. She had clammed up after that and then shown them both to the door. It had to mean something, but he couldn't force her to talk at this point. He'd called Ben to look into it on his way to the car.

"Harper is pretty feisty."

Eli wasn't ready to leave Julia's side, so he bought them dinner and drove her to the Capitol Building, where they could sit on the grass and eat. It wasn't the type of meal he'd use to try and impress a girl on a first date, but then he really wasn't supposed to be winning her over, so what exactly was he doing? Regardless, it was one of his favorite places in the city. Sitting in that park and watching the sunset was one of the ways he regrouped. Julia was stuck with him until he delivered her home.

Eli handed her a sandwich. She opened up the wax paper and smoothed it on the grass. Despite her long-sleeve shirt and scarf, she shuddered every now and then as if the faint, cool breeze was a little too chilly. Eli eased his suit jacket off and draped it around her shoulders.

"Are you sure you'll be warm enough?" Julia asked.

Eli opened his sandwich the same way. He popped open a bag of chips and split it between the two of them. "I'll be fine. From the look in your eye at the sandwich shop—you wanted some of these but just didn't want to ask for them."

She smiled. How he missed even the hint of it as both of them had defaulted to a business like interaction. Julia had been quiet most of the day and it bothered him more than he wanted it to. His mood lightened at the slightest contentment in hers. He didn't want to think about how much he would miss spending time with Julia when her case was over.

"You're right—it's just that the cheese dust is going to wreak havoc on my clothes and my breath."

Eli tapped his shirt pocket. "Always a few breath mints on hand."

Julia laughed and Eli's mood climbed even higher. "Really? I hadn't pegged you for a guy who keeps a stock of breath mints on hand."

"They're not necessarily always for me. Let's just say they make finishing some interviews a lot easier."

Julia nodded. "I get that. We use peppermint oil."

"At the hospital?"

"We put a little bit on cotton balls and stick it in rooms where the smell is not so pleasant. Same concept, I guess."

"I guess."

For a few minutes, both of them ate in silence. Eli felt like a salted slug on hot cement—his last energy reserves oozed into the grass. This morning, he could have run six miles and not blinked. Now every part of his body ached. His breath became short with mild exertion. Another good night's sleep in his own bed would do him good.

The next step. Quentin had messaged him and the Justice Department would allow him to interview Dr. Mark Heller. Should he take her? Would it be helpful if he did?

The sun hovered just above the mountain peaks. It was late—nearly eight o'clock. Was it obvious that Eli's delay in taking her home was to spend more time with her? Nestled in a small grove of nearby trees were a few extra agents helping to keep an eye out. No one seemed to be tailing them. For once, they'd had an uneventful day.

"What do you think of Harper?" Julia asked.

Eli swallowed the last bite of his sandwich and brushed the crumbs off his fingers. "She knows something. I think she knows you but won't say how."

Julia nodded, crumpling up her trash and putting it in the empty paper bag. "I agree."

"Problem is… I can't force her to confess what she knows and we don't have anything to leverage against her. My guess is she's the one who anonymously delivered the hit package to Ryder's parole officer. That probably saved your life, so even if a prosecutor came up with something to charge her with—a jury is going to have a lot of sympathy for her once she fesses up to that. Do you think you know Miles? If you knew and interacted with the family—even the cousin—it could be a piece to this puzzle."

Julia shook her head. "I didn't really feel like I'd met Miles before, but I feel like I know her. I used to be really good with faces before I was attacked. With her, I get that feeling, but I can't place it."

"Don't stress about it. I'm sure you come into contact with a lot of people. It would be impossible to remember them all…especially after what you went through."

"I've wanted to ask you something," Julia said. Why was it when a woman said that statement to Eli, it always sent his heart stammering? "Sure. Ask me anything."

"I want to see a doctor."

Eli turned to face her. What could be wrong? "For what?"

"I don't know if that's the right term. Not a medical doctor—a mental health professional. Someone who could help open up my memory and see if I can remember anything else about my attack."

"Julia—that can be a delicate process and we'd need to be very careful with how it's done. If the interviewer plants any sort of seed in your mind, then who knows if the information you provide is reliable? I'm sure you know as a nurse that the mind is one thing we haven't quite cracked. Eye-witnesses who wrongly identify a criminal but can pass a lie detector test. We don't want anything to get us off track."

"Are you sure that's it?"

"What?"

"That you just don't want us to get off track? Or is it you just don't want to see me suffer more psychological trauma in trying to remember?"

Was she right? Julia had as much vested interest as he did in remembering. If they did it the right way, there would be little fallout.

Eli focused on the mountains as he thought about her request. It was his favorite time of day when the sun drifted down below their peaks and shadowed them in varying hues of blue—almost flat. The view was deceptive. It made the grandeur of the mountains seem like a young child's painting.

What Eli was becoming more aware of from being in close proximity to Julia was how the traumatic things he saw affected him and how much he worked to deny it. Finding Julia so close to death had marked a point in time for him—an emotional burden he carried. Was he unwilling to allow her to suffer more pain just to save himself?

"Okay, I'll call someone I know. She retired last year, but is well respected in the field of forensic examination. I trust her."

"Great. It's settled, then."

Why was his heart dying when it was the happiest she'd been all day? "I'll call her tonight and see if I can get something set up for the morning. Let's get you home so you can get some sleep. See if we can have two uneventful nights in a row."

Julia relished being home. Even though just a few days had passed since she was here, it felt both foreign and welcoming at the same time.

"Everything checks out. I promise."

"Thanks, Ben," Julia said. "For everything. If you two don't mind, I'm going to bed. Tomorrow, I need to call to get replacements for my credit cards since my wallet is underwater. Who's up for going to the DMV with me?"

"I'd be happy to, Julia," Eli said. "Right after we meet with Dr. Powell."

"Dr. Powell?" Ben asked.

"Julia thought it would be a good idea for someone to jog her memory. Since she's been remembering some new details—why not see if a professional could help?" Eli said.

Ben frowned, looking at Julia. "You've been through so much, and memory is a tricky thing. What you remember might not be the truth, and we don't want to contaminate the case with any unnecessary details."

"Eli's already expressed his concern about it. I want to help get a quick resolution to this case. If you don't take me, I'll drive myself there."

A rush of tension burned in Julia's chest. The feeling wasn't unfamiliar to her. It was a rare event to confront a physician about an order that could harm a patient, but she felt the same in those instances as she did now.

Don't. Mess. With. Me.

She turned on her heel and marched up the stairs into the quiet cavern of her bedroom. After lighting several candles in her bathroom and soaking in the tub for a good thirty minutes, she started to feel the tension ease from her muscles. She dressed for bed and turned on her bedside lamp and pulled the covers down. From the bottom of the bed, she grabbed the black leather Bible that Eli gave her.

At first, a moment of grief washed over her as she opened the unmarred, crisp pages. All her notes, highlights, little doodles were waterlogged fish food. So much of her young life had been marked by grief. In her profession, she dealt with death—children dying, no less. Not daily, but too much. The loss of her memory. The loss of feeling safe and protected—and the hope that she and Eli could see if they were a good match together. Was she so broken that no man would ever want to be with her? The death of her parents. Not being able to contact her grandfather. Her Bible.

She opened the Bible to the New Testament and began to read, but frustration overwhelmed her.

A genealogy for Jesus. And hers was…severed.

She yanked open her nightstand drawer to pull out a package of gel highlighters. There were several notebooks there. As she rustled around, she found the journal where she'd make notes about the patients she'd cared for. Despite the potential patient privacy violation, it was a way for her to process the emotions she couldn't convey at work and no one knew about it or ever saw it.

No one appreciates a sobbing nurse who can't do her job. This is a way to safely decompress.

Setting the Bible aside, she grabbed the journal and opened it up. Some pages were wrinkled from her tears as she wrote about the death of a patient. She looked over some of her early entries from nursing school and smiled at what a novice she had been. One of her first patients on the medical unit was an elderly woman contracted into the fetal position and whose mouth gaped open but never spoke any words—her body ravaged by a stroke. Julia had stood there for the longest time trying to figure out how to get the blood pressure cuff on her arm when it was bent at ninety degrees. When she tried to ease the leathery muscles straight—it was evident the arm was not to be coaxed into any different position. Not knowing what else to do, Julia went and got her clinical instructor, who, without any qualms, threaded that blood pressure cuff around the elderly woman's arm and got the reading in about thirty seconds.

After reading a few entries, Julia got brave enough to look at the months that led up to her attack. Were there any clues here that could help her tomorrow during her interview with Dr. Powell? Would it be possible to recall these events, or was her mind so fractured that her past was inaccessible?

Journal entries from two months before her attack.

A newborn with sepsis. One of the most difficult cases to manage as a nurse in the pediatric ICU. So much needed to be done to save the baby's life. Multiple labs. Trying to ease tiny catheters into threadlike veins. This particular newborn, a baby girl just three weeks old, had rapidly deteriorated and been placed on a breathing machine.

Warm softness eased through Julia's body. In the middle of that crisis—of that baby almost dying—she remembered the respiratory therapist assigned that day. Brin was her name. After they had stabilized the patient, Brin placed her hand over the baby's forehead and said the sweetest prayer.

Lord, I ask Your blessing upon this child. That You would heal her tiny body. That You would let her grow up to experience the splendor You have created for her here. Amen.

Julia had been jealous of the freedom Brin had in expressing her faith at the bedside. What she had done had been a dangerous thing—if the family complained, she likely would have faced disciplinary action.

Brin.

Joyful. Full of life. The best, most sarcastic sense of humor.

Short. African American.

Julia pictured the woman in her mind. Her heart began to race. There was something her fingers itched to remember.

The hit package.

Julia threw her bedcovers aside and raced down the stairs in time to see Eli headed out the door.

He wasn't going to say goodbye?

"The hit package!" Julia cried. "I need to see it."

Eli walked back into the house. "Why?"

She implored Eli with her eyes. "Do you have a copy? Please, I need to look through the pages again."

Eli shook his head. "Not on me. Ben?"

"Sure—in my briefcase. Hold on."

Ben left Eli and Julia alone in the foyer.

"You were going to leave without saying goodbye?" The lump in her throat made it difficult to say the words in the nonchalant manner she wanted to present.

"I'm sorry. I didn't realize that would be important to you."

Why should it have been? Eli had made it clear they were only to interact in a professional way. Even then—it would have been polite to let her know. And what—was Ben staying overnight? Even though he'd spent most of the day there?

"I just thought..." She shook her head. Why get into this now? "You never told me what time I needed to be ready to meet this doctor in the morning."

"Right. We'll need to leave here by eight."

Ben handed her the manila envelope, and she opened it and skimmed through the pages. The photos that Eli had shown her of the other victims weren't there.

"I need to see the photos...of the other victims."

Ben shrugged. "I don't have a paper copy. We can probably find them on the internet."

Eli pulled his phone from his jacket and a few finger taps later he handed it to her. She scrolled through the faces.

Brin.

Julia thrust the phone toward Eli with Brin's picture. "I know her. We worked together."

Eli took the phone from her. "She's a respiratory therapist, but Children's didn't have any record of her being an employee."

"Then you didn't ask the right people or the person you talked to didn't know what he was talking about. She was from an agency—not employed by the hospital, but contracted to work for Children's when we were short-staffed."

"I don't know how this pertains to what's happening now," Ben said.

Eli put the phone back in his pocket. "I disagree. We didn't really know how the victims were tied together other than they were all medical professionals. We thought that was perhaps Dr. Heller's type, and he chose them based on that."

"And now?" Julia asked.

"If you know this person and you worked together, then perhaps we've thought about this case the wrong way. Maybe you weren't chosen by the Hangman because you were a medical professional, but based on where you worked. That would make more sense as far as his hunting ground goes. We know you and Mark Heller worked together, but we didn't find a significant tie to the hospital with the other victims. The victim found in Wyoming totally threw us off."

Eli scratched his head. "What this tells me is that we need to go back and verify whether the link could be the hospital and not just some random choosing of health-care workers like we thought before."

Ben smiled. "Good work, Julia. Did you suddenly remember this?"

"I used to keep a journal of the patients I cared for. I know with patient privacy and all that I probably shouldn't, but it's a way for me to process what happens."

"How long have you kept this journal?" Eli asked.

"Since I started nursing school."

"And when did you stop?"

"The day I was attacked."

"You didn't keep journaling when you went back to nursing?" Ben asked.

"Maybe I was dealing with too much just trying to survive the day to think about processing anything extra."

"Julia, would you mind if I looked through it tonight?" Ben asked. "I'll be up anyway and I'll see if I can find any more clues that could give us insight into your case."

Instinctually, she resisted Ben's suggestion. Of course, she wanted to do whatever she could to help solve this case. To get her freedom back. But there was too much there—her soul bared on the page. What would he think of her?

No, it was too much to ask.

"I'll—"

"Julia, it's okay. I can see your reluctance." Eli turned to Ben. "Let her look over it, and I'm sure she'll let us know if there's anything relevant. Tomorrow, after your appointment, we'll see if we can tie the victims together. Okay? Are we good here?"

Julia was. The look on Ben's face suggested otherwise.

TWELVE

Julia laid in bed watching the soft breeze caress and curl her curtains with a playful whimsy she wished she could swallow up to ease the pressure she felt in her chest. She missed Eli. Missed everything about him. His quirky half smile. The glimmer of his blue eyes. The feel of his soft lips against hers. Was there any hope for the two of them? Perhaps that was the benefit of her case going unsolved—she and Eli could be together. Even if they couldn't be together in the way she was beginning to dream and hope for.

Without warning, a concussive blast wave tore through the room. Heat surged on Julia's face before the sound of the explosion hit her eardrums. The rupture of light confused her. Shards of glass raked across her face as if she'd been slapped by a cactus.

She bolted up in bed. Wind blew unencumbered through her broken bedroom windows, her curtains in shreds from the glass that tore through the thin fabric propelled by the force of a fiery air mass displacing the quiet of the night. When Julia glanced out her window—all she could see was red-hot angry flames consuming the house next door.

Ben crashed through her door and ran to her bed, grabbing her by the shoulders and pulling her from the warmth of her covers.

Her mind reeled back to a moment in time she didn't want to relive. The same crash of a male form through her door and grabbing her—overpowering her and knocking her backward onto the floor, then…

She cocked her arm and with all her might swung her fist into the man's jaw.

This will not happen to me again.

The man backpedaled, rubbing his chin where her fist met his flesh. "Julia! It's Ben. The house next door…"

Julia brushed her fingertips over her face, collecting warm thick fluid. She blinked several times and came back to the present. "What's happening?"

Ben approached her more slowly, his hands raised yet reaching for her. The light from the flames next door illuminated the room enough that she could see Jace enter her bedroom, as well. "There's been an explosion. The house next door—is just gone. We need to evacuate you."

Julia's adrenaline-laced mind tried to make sense of what he was saying.

Her heart hammered in her ears.

Were her neighbors home?

Julia raced past the two men. She could hear Jace talking into his wrist mic behind her—notifying whoever was on the other side to dispatch 911 to their location. She heard Eli's name in the litany of commands he listed off with hastened breath. Julia's feet hit the steps, and she missed the last one, falling hard on the landing on her knees and elbows. Plywood still covered her picture window. As she clambered up the door to release the lock, Ben dropped his body weight on her legs—trapping her.

Bile raced up her throat and filled her mouth. Her mind switched to her old house. A shadowy figure trapped her legs there, too. She kicked, hard—a foot getting loose and connecting with the man's face.

"Julia, what is the matter with you!" Ben yelled. "We need to evacuate."

She scrambled to her feet, swallowing several times to clear the cool rush of saliva from her mouth. She threw the dead bolt open.

"You can't go out there without us." Ben reached for her, and she backed up to the door.

Jace cleared the staircase. Julia turned and yanked the door open. After rushing a few steps outside, she saw Mrs. Jones and her son, Levi, lying on their front lawn.

Even at this distance it felt as if the flames would melt the flesh from her bones. Charging past Ben back into her house, she rushed into her kitchen and grabbed a toolbox from underneath her sink.

What it contained was a far cry from the hammer and screwdrivers most men carried—it was her personal trauma kit, and she needed it now.

Ben rushed in behind her and blocked her from exiting the kitchen. His chest heaved. "Julia—you have to listen to me. I don't want to detain you, but you're not leaving."

You're not leaving.

Those same words. How was it possible? Julia withered to her knees, her body shaking so badly she couldn't make sense of what was happening.

Whatever caused the explosion next door—it was triggering memories from her attack. She pulled the toolbox toward her and stood up on shaky legs. "I'm going next door. You and Jace can either help or get out of my way. If you detain me, I'll hire a lawyer and file charges against you. I'm not your prisoner!"

Ben's eyes widened. He tossed his hands in the air and stepped aside. Somehow, even with jellyfish legs, she rushed by him and down her porch steps.

She positioned herself between Mrs. Jones and

her son and threw the lid open on her first aid kit.
Levi—the definition of a towhead blond if there
ever was one—was crying, his hand clutching a
piece of glass that punctured the right side of his
chest. His mother lay crumpled on the ground
next to him, unmoving.

Julia placed a calming hand on his forehead.
"Levi, it's Miss Julia. Is your dad home?"

He threw his head side to side—the pain a muz-
zle to his words.

One good thing. If someone was still inside
their house, they would be beyond rescue.

"I'm going to help you, but I need to check on
your mom first."

He continued to cry. Ben and Jace hovered next
to her, uncertainty clouded their faces. Jace had
a gun drawn and scanned the area like a hawk
looking for prey.

"Ben, you're a certified first responder, right?"

He nodded and kneeled down next to her.

"I need to get her on her back so I can see if
she's breathing, but I need to protect her spinal
cord. Can you help me logroll her?"

Julia scurried to the woman's head and placed
her hands on either side of her neck. Ben reached
across her body and placed a hand on her hip and
shoulder.

"On three."

Ben nodded and Julia counted out loud. In one
seamless motion they eased her onto her back.

Blood dripped from the woman's ears. Julia settled her cheek over her mouth. A soft, panting breath puffed against her skin. She placed two fingers in the side of the woman's neck.

A pulse was present.

"She's breathing with a decent pulse. Not much we can do for her until rescue gets here."

Walking on her knees to Levi, she grabbed a pair of trauma sheers from her first aid box. Quickly, she cut up the middle of his shirt and through each sleeve and lifted the fabric from his chest. A large glass shard was embedded in his chest on the right side—near the base of his lung. Blood oozed at a steady pace from the wound. Julia threw on a pair of gloves, handed a set to Ben and grabbed a package that held several square pieces of gauze.

"Put the gloves on and then place these around the glass and press. We need to control the bleeding."

Ben pulled the gloves on and did as instructed. Pulling the top tray from her kit, Julia found her old stethoscope in the bottom from nursing school. She laid the stethoscope's bell against Levi's chest. She could hear breath sounds even to the base of the right lung.

She sat back on her heels, relief flooding through her.

The glass seemingly hadn't punctured the lung,

but it could have cut through his liver, which would lead to rapid blood loss if not controlled.

She smoothed her fingers through his hair. "Levi, things will be okay. Breathe with me." Julia inhaled deeply and held her breath.

Levi tossed his head side to side. "It hurts!"

Ben continued to stack gauze around the shard of glass to stabilize it and began to secure them down with wide swaths of medical tape.

Julia reached for his hand "I know, but you're so brave. Everything is going to be okay."

"What about my mom?" he cried.

Julia's heart tore open. It was a basic tenet of pediatric nursing that children were never lied to. There was always the balance of telling the truth without provoking more anxiety. She settled her hand against his cheek. "She's injured but breathing."

Sirens...finally. The whoosh and squeal of brakes. A small army of firefighters dressed in bunker gear disembarked from three trucks. Their reflective stripes made them look like disembodied stick figures dancing. Three men grabbed fire hoses from the back of the truck. Two at the nearest fire hydrant. An ambulance screeched to a halt and a paramedic team dressed in navy blue slacks and white shirts pulled a gurney from the back.

Three other firefighters neared Julia and Ben on the lawn. "What do we have?"

"This is Deanna Jones. Approx forty-five. I

found her on the lawn. She's unconscious but has a pulse and is breathing." Julia motioned to the boy. "This is her son, Levi. He has a large piece of glass in his chest that we've stabilized in place to control the bleeding."

The firefighter peeled his hat off. "What about you?" He reached toward Julia's face.

In her haste to help her neighbors, she'd forgotten the blood she felt on her own face. "I'm fine—really."

A black car squealed to a halt at the base of her driveway and Eli bolted from it, his hand on his weapon as he closed the distance between them.

Ben stood up from where he'd been kneeling next to the boy as the firefighters took over his care.

"What happened?" Eli asked.

"It's like I told you—the neighbor's house just exploded." Water gushed through the firefighter's hoses. Julia's mouth dried as she saw small areas where her roof was burning. Another hose began streaming water to the side of her house and onto the roof itself—water pouring through her shattered bedroom windows.

Eli grabbed Julia's elbow. "You're coming with me."

She yanked her arm free. "I'm going to the hospital with Deanna and Levi. She doesn't have any family here, and no one will be there for Levi until she wakes up or his father arrives."

Eli grabbed her arm again and pulled her close, his hand behind her neck, his lips hot against her as his breath funneled into her ear. "You will come with me. Right. Now."

The intensity of his words scared her, and suddenly the gravity of the situation hit her like a wrecking ball. Jace continued to scope the area. Ben nodded at her, confirming Eli's directive.

Her knees softened, and she bent over to ease the light-headedness. Was this her fault? Had her mere presence in her own home put these people's lives at risk?

Eli hurriedly guided her to his car. Moments after she secured her seat belt, Eli peeled out down the street.

"Where are we going?"

"The only place I know that is truly safe—my house."

Eli gripped his steering wheel so tight that his hands ached, his eyes laser-focused on the road in front of them. He made a covert check of the rearview mirror every few seconds. At four o'clock in the morning, there wasn't much traffic, a blessing because it would be easier to tell if someone was following them.

So far, so good.

Julia sat as still as a hunted animal in hiding. The blank stare in her eyes petrified. What could he say to lessen what she was feeling? The truth was she now realized how diabolically intent the hit man was on collecting his money.

Four incidents in the span of four days. It was a pattern. What disturbed Eli more was that he couldn't rule out someone on Julia's detail being involved. At a minimum, someone had to be feeding the hit man information on their whereabouts. Had Julia's hit man accidentally gotten the wrong house? What member of Eli's team could be involved? The same agent had not been present at all four events, and at each event every agent had a partner with him. Was it someone from the office?

Eli arched his shoulders and tried to ease the muscle soreness. Was this paranoia? Even though he was convinced none of these instances were accidental, why would someone on his team be involved? If they were, how were they connected to the Hangman?

Parking his car in his driveway, he said, "Stay here until I come and get you."

He slid from the vehicle and paced to the other side. Keeping a hand on his gun, he pulled the door open and reached for Julia's hand. She willingly took his hand, and he escorted her up the stairs to his third-story apartment.

Eli led her into the kitchen and settled her on a bar stool by his kitchen counter. Reaching for her chin, he pulled it up until her eyes met his. Tears streamed down her cheeks, and he felt his eyes moisten in response.

Please, Lord. Help me ease her pain. Let me do and say the right thing.

"Does anything hurt? Should I have taken you to the hospital?"

Almost imperceptivity, she shook her head at his statement.

He left her and moistened a towel with warm water. When he circled back, he wiped the blood and tears from her face. He grit his teeth against a desire to plant soft kisses where the glass had parted skin.

As gently as he could, he washed the dried crimson crust from her face. There were also cuts to the side of her neck, hands and feet. "What else should I do to treat these? They're small cuts. I don't think you need stitches."

"Antibiotic ointment."

He was relieved to have some on hand. Gathering what he needed, he returned to her quickly. Placing small gobs on the end of a Q-tip, he brushed the ointment over her injuries.

Eli placed his hands on her knees. "Julia, please talk to me. I can't take this silence."

Her lips trembled, and all his work to clear her tears was undone.

Though he'd promised himself he wouldn't cross a professional line, he gathered her in his arms and held her against him. After countless minutes, he could feel her heart beat less erratically against his chest. The tension in her muscles eased to the point where it became difficult to differentiate her body from his. He stroked her hair, breathing in its soft citrus scent.

Julia fit perfectly against him. His father always told him when he found a girl whose body melted against his own like a missing puzzle piece—she was the one God designed to be his forever.

When her trembling stopped, he reluctantly eased back.

"Don't leave me again," she said.

"I promise, I won't."

Julia smoothed her hair from her eyes. "Something happened after the explosion. I remembered more. It was all mixed in with Ben trying to get me out of the house."

"Did you see your assailant?"

"Just part of the attack."

"What's best for you right now? Considering what's happened—do you still feel like seeing the psychologist in the morning?"

"Absolutely, it's time to stop this creep. I'll do whatever it takes to end this."

And Eli resolved to do whatever it took to keep her safe—even if it meant his life.

THIRTEEN

After Eli settled Julia down enough for her to get a few hours of sleep in his guest room, Ben stopped by unannounced. In his hand was a grocery bag full of Julia's clothes. He offered it to Eli as some sort of peace offering.

They sat briefly at Eli's kitchen table. The sun was just peeking over the horizon, dispelling the darkness and evil that attempted to consume Julia in the night.

"There's significant destruction to Julia's home. Not a total loss, but she'll be displaced for months. Water damage—mostly to the side that faced the home that exploded. Major roof damage. Windows blown out. Firefighters kept her home from burning to the ground, but…"

Eli sat and waited for him to continue. Even though Eli hadn't been with the marshals' service long, he'd never had so much go awry with a witness in such a short amount of time.

Ben continued. "I looked for the journal she

kept, and found it in her nightstand table. It's significantly water-damaged—hard to even see the words she wrote. I don't know how useful it will be in offering clues about the Hangman and his other victims."

"Where is it?" Eli asked.

"I put it in the FBI evidence locker. I figured that would be the safest place for it."

Eli nodded. Ben was probably right on that account. Over the coming days, there'd be, at the very least, insurance investigators traipsing through her house doing a damage assessment.

Eli could only assess the physical damage Julia was suffering—the displacement, the loss of her home and belongings. Two Bibles that she had a deep personal connection with. The emotional and psychological toll was immeasurable. Every person had a breaking point. Where was Julia's? Had they already crossed it?

"I might have a bit of good news," Ben said.

Eli opened the grocery bag and was overwhelmed by a smoky odor. He'd have to get these in the wash before Julia woke up. He didn't want her to suffer any more trauma.

"A neighbor had a security camera that shows a man entering the Joneses' residence a few minutes before the explosion. We think it's Ryder."

Eli retied the flimsy plastic bag. "That doesn't make any sense. What, he gets the wrong house?"

Ben shook his head. "It makes perfect sense to

me. He knows we're protecting her, so a full-on assault at the house isn't going to work. Blowing up the house next door has the potential to kill two birds with one stone."

"Which two?" Eli asked.

"Julia and the…" Ben paused and clamped his lips closed. "Us."

"It's so risky. Plus, it endangered the lives of two other people. By the way, how are they?"

"That's the bright spot. The mother had a skull fracture, which caused the bleeding from her ears and unconsciousness, but she's awake and talking. The son had an operation to remove that nasty piece of glass, but otherwise he did well. Both are expected to make a full recovery. Aurora Fire was investigating it as arson even before the video revealed someone entering the house. The husband is on his way back from a business meeting in New York."

Another curious fact. The father, perhaps the only defense shield the family had, was out of town.

"What's your plan?" Ben asked.

"Julia's adamant about going through with this forensic interview. I got a hold of Kathleen, and she was able to move the interview to later today so Julia could sleep in—if she's even sleeping."

"Good. Hopefully, she'll be able to remember something, because I feel like as long as this guy is out there, none of us are going to be getting any sleep."

"I've got Julia covered today. Maybe Will or Jace can help me tonight so I can sleep. I want you over at Julia's house eavesdropping on the fire investigation. Work with your FBI cohorts and do whatever you can to find this Ryder character and bring him in."

"There's a BOLO for Ryder. Every cop in the city is looking for him." Ben headed to the front door. "I'll keep you informed."

Eli tried to get a few hours of sleep, but his restless mind caused the same reaction to his physical state. All he knew when Julia emerged from the guest bedroom was just how uncomfortable his couch was and how long it took a few clothes to be washed and dried.

"Tea?" Eli asked Julia.

"Absolutely."

She sat at the table just as he left it. He warmed up the griddle and pulled the pancake batter out of the refrigerator.

"Your pumpkin spice creamer is a little out of season, but I thought caramel had your name all over it."

"You'd be right," Julia said. "You didn't have to go to all this trouble. I would have been fine with cereal."

Eli set a steaming mug in front of her. "After

the night you've had, I think you deserve to be spoiled. Bacon and eggs?"

"Even better."

That was what Eli liked—a woman with a good appetite who wasn't shy about eating in front of a man. He spooned a full ladle of batter onto the grill, cracked a couple of eggs and put the already cooked bacon in the microwave to heat up.

"Ben stopped by a few hours ago."

"I figured," Julia said, pulling on the front of her shirt. "I have to give him marks for putting together clothing ensembles better than you can."

Eli laughed. "True, but he didn't wash, dry and fold them like I did." It was also good to see she could maintain a sense of humor in the middle of a crisis. "We each have our gifts."

"Do you like Ben?" Julia asked.

Eli flipped the pancakes over. Why would she ask such a question? Was she picking up on some of Eli's suspicions about his team? "We haven't worked together very long. It's a unique partnership. After your case is wrapped up, we'll go our separate ways."

"So you've said. It's partly why I'm asking."

"What do you think of him?"

Julia shrugged. "I don't know."

"I doubt that." Eli plopped the pancakes and an egg onto her plate adding a couple of pieces of warmed bacon from the microwave. "You're a woman and a nurse. Your intuition must be off the charts." He placed butter and syrup on the table before setting their plates down in front of them.

As he grabbed his fork, Julia put her hand over his to still it. "Do you mind if I pray? I just—"

Eli set his utensils down. "No, I'd like that." Folding his hands he lowered his head even though what he wanted to do was keep his eyes on her. Something so foreign to him strangely felt right in her presence.

"Father, I thank You for keeping me, Ben and Jace safe last night. I pray for Deanna and Levi— that You would bring them to a full recovery. I thank You for Eli. For his keeping me safe and for…"

Her voice trailed, and Eli snuck one eye open. What was she censoring herself from saying?

"Amen."

Eli clenched his eye closed so she wouldn't catch him stealing a glance. "Amen."

Julia tore into her pancakes with a vengeance. "I'll take your statement about women as a compliment. As far as Ben is concerned, I just have the feeling he's not totally on the level."

"In what way?" Eli asked.

"I feel like he's hiding something."

"Everyone has their secrets."

Julia set her fork down and grabbed her cup of tea. "I'm starting to wonder if those secrets have any bearing on my case."

* * *

Dr. Kathleen Powell's home was a master's-style bungalow eerily similar to the one Julia had been attacked in. Her color choices were vastly different from Julia's taste, which made it easier to be there.

Eli stayed a protective two feet behind her. After he put his suit on, earpiece in and wrist mic on, it was as if his persona changed to the überprofessional agent. All he needed was the reflective sunglasses, and he'd fit the stereotype of the government law enforcement officer on TV.

Kathleen's gray hair was cut short in a smart pixie style. Her blue eyes, a shade darker than Eli's ice blue, portrayed warmth that immediately put Julia at ease. After giving Eli a grandmotherly hug, she took Julia by the hand and escorted her into a cozy room with two overstuffed chairs and a small love seat.

"Julia, please make yourself comfortable."

She sat on the love seat, and Dr. Powell took a seat across from her on a chair.

"I'm just going to do a quick house and perimeter check. I'll be right back," Eli said.

Julia watched him until she couldn't see him anymore. It unnerved her to not have him in her line of sight.

Kathleen cleared her throat to pull Julia's attention her way. "Julia, I understand from Eli you had a very rough night."

Julia folded her hands tightly in her lap. "You know, under normal circumstances it would probably be more than I could take, but in light of recent incidents…"

"Like crashing into a river and saving two people?"

Julia smiled. "It's all about your perspective. I've lost a lot of things in this past week—mostly physical things that can be replaced, but I'm alive, my grandfather is alive and that's what matters most."

"You said *mostly* physical things."

"Yes."

"That would leave room for something you've lost that doesn't match that criteria. I'm just wondering what that is."

Julia bit her lower lip. *Now I know why Eli likes Kathleen so much—she can delve deep without really seeming to.* "I lost my Bible in the river. And a journal I kept for years, I'm presuming, was destroyed by water damage last night. Since I have amnesia, it's painful to lose things that can replace the memories I lost—especially of my parents."

Kathleen grabbed a piece of paper. "That must be very hard."

"I've been through worse. I'll get over it."

Kathleen nodded and made a few scrawls on the notepad she kept. "Let me explain what our purpose is here today so we both have the same expectations." She set her pen down and squared her gaze on Julia. "Eli tells me that you want to undergo a forensic interview to help you remember details of your attack."

"Exactly."

"Have you ever been through anything like this before?"

"No."

"You didn't partake in any sort of counseling after your attack?"

Julia shook her head. "I didn't have any memory of it, and I was too busy trying to rebuild my life to take the time to do it."

"Eli tells me you think you've remembered some details."

"He's right, but I can never really see the attacker's face. That's what I'm hoping you can help me with."

"Before you started to get these flashes of your assailant, do you think you've had any mental health issues that pertain to this traumatic event in your life? Anxiety? Symptoms of post-traumatic stress disorder?"

Julia's neck ached. Was she truly ready for this? "I don't like to be restrained or confined. Really tight places give me the creeps."

"That makes sense to me on several levels."

Julia settled her hand over her throat. "Can we just focus on why I'm here?"

Kathleen set her pen down. "Considering your circumstances, I am willing to do that, but I want to encourage you to see someone when this crisis is over—and it will be over. I have every faith in Eli that this man will be brought to justice. But I think for you to be whole again, it would be helpful for you to confront what's happened. Even though your memory is patchy, this incident had a heavy emotional impact, and managing that will only make you stronger."

Julia considered her statement. Health-care professionals were the worst at caring for themselves, and Julia was no different. "I will. I promise."

Eli returned to the small living room. "All clear. Where's the best place for me to be?"

"Can Eli stay?" Julia asked.

"Yes, with your permission, but I'll only allow it if you don't censor what you're going to say. If you feel like Eli's presence will inhibit our goal for today, I'll put him elsewhere."

Julia knew in her heart that she could be open in front of Eli. Above everything else, she didn't want to hide anything from him. "It's better for me if he's here."

Eli bowed his head and took the chair next to Kathleen.

"And, Eli—you need to be silent. I don't want you putting any extra pressure on Julia to come up with an answer. We don't want her mind filling in any details that aren't true in an effort to be helpful to the police."

"Understood." He smiled at Julia. "It's going to be okay, I promise."

"Great. Julia, what I'm going to do is walk you through the attack, but we're not going to start on that right away. I'd like to start with the week before this incident. Let's get your memory warmed up, primed to this time frame. What do you remember on the days leading up to this event?"

Julia snuggled into the corner of the couch and grabbed one of the throw pillows to hold in front of her body. "I remember it was a hard week at work."

"How was it difficult?"

"I was working in the pediatric ICU then. We had a run of deaths. Some odd things had been happening in the unit over the last several months and there was a feeling among the nurses that we had a black cloud hovering. We were waiting…"

Julia's voice trailed, her mind drifted back to those beds. The children she had cared for. "Waiting for what?" Kathleen asked.

"For the third death," Julia said.

"What does that mean?" Kathleen asked.

"Deaths usually come in threes."

Kathleen nodded. "So there were two previous deaths close together?"

"I don't know how to explain it. We had our *usual* code events. Children we tried desperately to save but, in our hearts, knew the probability of their survival was nil. These incidents, though hard, were expected and easier to deal with. But we'd also had a run of what the hospital terms sentinel events."

"Explain that to me."

"A sentinel event is a patient death that occurs in the hospital as the result of a medical error."

"And there had been two such deaths?" Kathleen clarified.

"Yes. All this is confidential, right?"

"Absolutely. You can talk about your patients here."

Julia glanced Eli's way. "Same here," he said.

"One patient, a preteen around twelve, died from equipment failure."

"What type of equipment?" Kathleen asked.

"His ventilator malfunctioned. It was a new type the hospital was trialing. The machine delivered successive breaths without allowing the air to come out and it blew out both his lungs. He never recovered."

"The other incident?"

"A medication error. A patient received a fatal dose of potassium."

"How did that happen?"

"A nurse placed an incorrect weight in a patient's chart. She accidentally entered it in pounds instead of kilograms, making the child significantly heavier. When the doctor placed the potassium order, the pharmaceutical safety systems that catch potential medication errors didn't trigger because the dose was correct for the inputted weight, but toxic for that child."

"What was the staff feeling?"

"Horrified. Uneasy. We were all feeling scrutinized. The administration was on the unit all the time. Lawyers became involved in each of these cases. I cared for the boy who died as a result of the ventilator malfunction during the shift when he succumbed to the complications of that event and I knew I was going to face a deposition in the case—at some point."

"Whether or not you felt responsible for this boy's death is not the reason you're here today—we'll set it aside for now, but I want you know that I think it's a worthy avenue to explore."

The pressure within Julia's chest rose. Even if she wasn't directly responsible for the boy's death, she had been his nurse, and nursing was all about advocating for patients. Nursing wasn't about being doctors' handmaids and blindly carrying out their orders. Part of her job was educating families about the doctor's medical plan and helping families weigh the choices presented by the doctor, then circling back to the physician with any concerns the family had.

"What were the deaths that happened just prior to your attack?"

"One was related to child abuse and the other a child with a malformed heart."

"Expected but tough."

"Always."

"Before we get into what happened on the day of your attack, Eli explained to me that you have amnesia related to your brain being deprived of oxygen as a result of the hanging."

Julia pulled her knees into her chest. "That's right."

"To me, it explains the period of amnesia after the injury—when you were so sick in the hospital and into some of your rehab time. But your mind was fully functional when this person came into your house, correct?"

"That's true, but—"

Kathleen continued. "I know the brain is the organ we understand the least and amnesia is even trickier, but what I will say is that I believe you have a full recording in your mind as to what happened during this event and there may be several factors as to why you've closed it off, but *it's there.*"

Julia tried to swallow over the lump in her throat. All the bravado in the world could melt away when someone was confronted with what they had promised to do—no matter how sincere they were at the time.

"Let's start with what you remember about that day."

"I just got up and was getting ready to work my third day shift in a row. It was around five o'clock."

"Did you have a routine that you followed before work?"

"I would usually do some devotion time and then get in the shower."

"Is that what happened on this day?"

Julia closed her eyes. She'd just come downstairs, dressed in her scrubs, about to put her shoes on… "I got a phone call."

"From who?"

"A neighbor. Harriet Wilson. She's an elderly woman who lived next door to me."

How could Julia have forgotten this?

"What did she want?"

"Eggs."

Kathleen scratched a few notes on her pad. What could be so important about eggs? "Was it unusual for Harriet to call you?"

Julia smoothed her hands over her face. "She had some health issues. I was helping her— keeping tabs on her. I'd shovel her walk when it snowed. Make sure she was okay when it got too hot. That sort of thing."

"So she'd call you on occasion with these sorts of requests."

Julia reached back in her memory to her interactions with Harriet. Most often they discussed Harriet's medical problems. An issue every nurse faced was people offering too much personal information about themselves. Harriet didn't have any close relatives. Her siblings were dead, and she never married.

Harriet wasn't a woman to bake or cook...ever.

"My neighbor never asked me for ingredients before. I'm not sure she could cook. Plus, it was early in the morning and she was a late riser."

"Did Harriet request anything else?"

"She said she'd walk over and get them."

Another odd statement. Julia's eyes searched Eli's—it was as if he was keeping them directed away from her, trying to diminish his presence.

"Harriet had dysfunctional mobility. She could walk with assistance but rarely ventured from her house. Her church was delivering meals, and every so often, I'd run by to see if she needed any food. I always bought things that were easy to put together. Cereal. Sandwich makings. Microwave dinners. Definitely not the healthiest, but I knew she wouldn't starve."

"What happened after the phone call?"

"Someone knocked on my door."

Kathleen looked at Eli, and he shifted uncomfortably in his seat. Was his being present too much for him? Or was he feeling what she now knew—that the person at the door wasn't her neighbor? That it had all been a ruse?

"You said *someone*, but you were expecting Harriet. Why do you think you said that?"

Julia folded her hands together, bending her fingers back to help ease the ache that spread from her neck all the way down her arms. She couldn't differentiate if the increasing pain was soreness from the car accident or physical distress at confronting this emotional trauma. "I was surprised."

"At what?"

"That she could make it to my door so quickly."

"Were you feeling anything else?"

Julia saw herself walking to her front door. The impatient, successive knocks. Relentless pounding. "I'm scared."

"Why?" Kathleen asked.

Julia became light-headed. The sound of blood rushing in her ears like a tornado she couldn't stop.

Just breathe. You can do this. You have to do this.

"Can you feel your feet on the floor?" Kathleen asked.

Julia pressed her feet into the carpet.

Stay here. Stay in this moment. He can't hurt you.

She wanted to look at Eli but couldn't let herself fall into that emotional well of confusion.

Lord, You are the only one right now who can help me do this. Help me remember. Help me stop this person so I can have my life back.

Kathleen's voice. "This is a safe place, Julia. Nothing bad is going to happen to you here."

Julia exhaled slowly. "I'm thinking it's not Harriet at the door."

"What else?"

"I'm calling out Harriet's name, and she's not answering me. But this person *will not* stop knocking on my door."

The pounding in Julia's temples matched that sound—the echo like a cannon firing. She pressed her fingers to her forehead to counteract the pain.

"Breathe with me, Julia. In through your nose like you're smelling flowers and then exhaling through your mouth like you're blowing out candles."

Julia hadn't realized how quick her breathing was, but she felt the tingle setting into her hands from hyperventilating. She closed her eyes and did as Kathleen instructed. "I go to the door. I'm thinking maybe something happened to Harriet and someone else is trying to get help for her, but…"

"What are you physically feeling?"

Julia pressed her hand against her chest. *You have to stay in this moment. You have to open this door. You have to see who it is that almost killed you.* "My heart is racing. I feel like I can't breathe."

"What happens next?"

"I grab the key and put it in the lock, turn it and put my hand on the doorknob."

"And?"

"A man shoves his way into my house. I'm so close to the door that it knocks me over."

Julia's eyes popped open, flitting around the room until locking with Eli's.

"You're okay, Julia. I'm here," Eli said. "I'm not leaving you."

His reassurance gave her strength in unexpected ways. *There's nothing I can't do as long as he's with me. What happens when this time is over and he has to move on? Can I bear it?*

"I try to crawl away, but this man is grabbing at my legs and pulling me toward him. I break free once and try to stand, but my socked feet slip on the hardwood floor—"

And then, just as quickly as Julia felt strength, it leached from her like sand through water. Pain flared in her chest like a lit piece of dynamite. Her breath came in short staggered gasps. She grabbed her knees and lowered her head, trying to convince her body what her mind knew, and she began to rock.

Your heart is not dying. This is just a panic attack. You can...no you will overcome it. You have to get control back. Lord, give my mind peace— let me see his face.

Eli stood from his chair and faced Kathleen. "She's been through enough. You have to stop. It's too much."

Through the noisy rush of static in her ears, Julia could hear Kathleen's voice, quite a bit lower than Eli's, pulling her from the throes of fear her body has trapped her in.

"Julia, slow your breathing down. This is not happening now. Just freeze the picture in your mind and slow down what's happening. What does the man do next?"

Julia clenched her teeth and slowed the scene down—advancing it frame by frame.

In between strobe-like flashes she got glimpses of her attacker's features. Striking green eyes. Long, dark hair tied back in a ponytail. Never one clear look at his face. He made one final grab for both her legs and yanked her backward. Her fingers clawed into the floor—and then he planted both knees in the middle of her back. She tried to twist her body to throw him off, but he inched higher—her arms unable to reach and grab any part of him.

Then a rag was smashed to her face—a sickingly sweet smell. Julia slithered her hands underneath her and in one last attempt to save her life—she pushed up and threw him to the right, into the wooden spindles of her staircase, but then blackness tunneled her vision.

"That's the last I remember."

Julia placed her elbows on her knees and smoothed her hands over her face to coax her heart into beating at a slower rate. Eli stood from his chair and neared her, placing his hand on her back and rubbing her tense muscles.

His touch was exactly what she needed. The faint sound of a phone vibrating pulled his spare hand to the inner pocket of his suit jacket for his phone.

"What is it?" Julia asked.

"They found him—Ryder Dymond. He's in police custody."

FOURTEEN

After the interview, Eli knew exactly the next step he needed to take, but he also knew Julia needed a break. He had taken her out for some distraction to the only place where he could unwind after a long day—an ice cream parlor. Giving her space to decompress after her forensic exam was just as important as letting her in on his game plan.

Julia sat before him, more playing than eating her mint chocolate chip with a hefty dose of fudge smearing the top. In her eyes, he could see the blackness that consumed her during her retelling of her attack still lingering. She settled her hand on the table, and he clasped his hand over hers, caressing the back of her hand with this fingertips.

"What are you thinking?" Eli asked.

Julia sniffed hard, pulling her hand away and grabbing her napkin to wipe her nose. "Just what a miserable failure I am. My big plan to help break this case wide-open didn't do you any good. I never got a good look at his face. Or if I did it's frozen and my mind won't let me remember it."

Eli pushed her ice cream bowl to the side and grabbed her hand, pressing it between his own. "That's not true. You don't know how valuable the information is that you shared."

"How can you say that?"

"I want to propose a plan to you. I'll need your help, but I think it will help us find out who this man is."

Julia looked skyward, her eyes closed. "Eli—"

He wanted to press her fingers against his lips, kissing them once with all the tenderness he felt in his heart. Could one kiss portray all that he felt toward her? He resigned himself to the fact that he was emotionally over the cliff for Julia, but if he could keep those feelings from spilling over into a physical expression, then maybe he could keep it hidden from her. With every ounce in him he didn't want to cross over his professional ethics again like when he'd kissed her at the doctor's cabin—at least until this case was over—but he knew his toe constantly broached the chalked white foul line.

"Your account gave us a lot to work with. I want to go back and interview your neighbor Harriet. Perhaps she can describe this man to a sketch artist, and we'd have something to work from. We also need to go back to your old house. Based on what you said, I know there could be forensic evidence your assailant left behind. We need to examine that staircase railing to see if there's any DNA evidence the first forensic sweep might have missed." Eli took a couple of quick bites of ice cream. "You also provided insight into how he incapacitated his victims enough to hang them. Chloroform is known to have the sweet smell you describe and can incapacitate someone by smothering their face. Old-school but effective."

"The more you talk, the more it sounds like you think the Hangman is not in prison."

Eli set his ice cream dish down. "I don't know if I would go that far. It's hard to refute the DNA evidence of Dr. Heller's blood in the rope fibers of each noose."

"Except Evelyn Roush."

"This leads me more to suspect the Hangman was working in partnership with someone who is trying to finish what they started."

"But why is he doing this?"

"Once we know that, a lot of things will become clear. Figuring out motives isn't as simple in real life as it is on television."

"Those are good ideas, but what if we just end up at the same place we are now?"

"All we can do is try. Let's call Harriet and see if she'll visit with us in the morning. Then I'll schedule a forensic team to meet us at your old house tomorrow afternoon and I'll have a little chat with Ryder Dymond."

"How did they find him?" Julia asked.

"Aurora police picked him up not far from your house. We'll see if he says anything. At this point he's not under arrest, but we can hold him for a few days for questioning."

Julia pulled her hands away. "You know what I can't get out of mind?"

"What?"

"That the man who tried to kill me didn't care if I saw his face. That's how sure he was that I was going to die."

Eli thought a lot about that fact, too. And the truth was, this memory of Julia's put her life more at risk because now she could potentially identify him. Whoever this man was, he was running out of time whether he was the true Hangman or not.

The next morning, Eli drove with Julia to Harriet Wilson's house. Seeing her old neighborhood brought back welcome memories. Julia relished recalling sitting on the porch of her home and watching the activity of her neighbors. Children playing ball in the street. Every Coloradoan owned a dog, and the parade of pet owners and their furry charges was always entertainment.

When Eli turned the corner on her street, a sense of foreboding overtook Julia.

They parked and Julia's eyes wandered over to her house. The property remained for sale, and her Realtor had agreed to meet them there in another thirty minutes, along with an FBI Forensics team, to take a second look for evidence. Could today hold clues they needed to bring this nightmare to an end?

"You really think this old lady is going to remember something?" Will asked from the backseat, fidgeting with the computer in his lap.

"What can it hurt? I don't see you or Ben coming up with any new ideas."

"Because our primary focus isn't investigation—it's protecting Julia," Ben said. "Since Quentin seems to have no interest in keeping you in line and protecting the U.S. Marshals' reputation, then it falls to me."

Why was he picking this moment to seemingly start a fight with two of his fellow agents?

Eli turned to Julia. "I'm going to let you take the lead on this. See if she remembers you and we'll go from there."

Julia exited the car and walked to the door, flanked by Eli and Ben with Will trailing a few steps behind. She knocked—several louder than normal raps. Ms. Wilson was a little hard of hearing.

Before long, a nose peeked through the crack, which widened to reveal a pair of milky brown eyes. They widened in surprise and the woman threw the door open.

"My sweet Julia! It really is you." Her bulky frame stepped onto the porch, and she pressed

Julia's face between her hands and then kissed her forehead. "I thought I was dreaming last night when that young man called me and said you wanted to come by for a visit."

"I have three men with me. Is it okay for all of us to come in?"

"Oh, of course. It's been so long since I've had a gentleman caller—imagine three in the same day."

The four of them stepped into the foyer. Eli held his hand out. "I'm the one who spoke to you on the phone."

Harriet dropped her hand onto Eli's shoulder. "What a fine specimen you are. It's nice to see that Julia found such a handsome man to take care of her."

"We're not together," they said in unison.

Julia's heart stalled. What did they say about protesting too loudly?

"This is Ben Murphy and Will Sullivan," Julia said.

Will stepped forward, his laptop clutched under one arm. "Nice to meet you," he said, shaking her hand briefly.

"You—" she pointed a finger straight at Ben's face "—look like someone I know." She tapped her index finger against her temple. "Have we met before?"

"Ms. Wilson, I'm afraid I've never had the pleasure of your company. Some say I look like Robert Downey Jr. Do you like his movies?" Ben asked.

As she clapped her hands together, her eyes held his—raptured by his presence. "That's it! You do look a lot like him, but I'm thinking of an older Hollywood actor." She snapped her fingers in the air. "I just can't place his name. Oh, it's going to keep me up all night thinking about this. Those green eyes of yours…really striking."

Ben bowed slightly. "It's the best compliment I could receive. My son…" His voice trailed. "Forgive me, I'm not really here to share personal stories. I'll let Julia explain the reason behind our visit."

Julia cataloged the moment in her mind. One thing about Ben—he wanted to remain a closed book. Was that unusual? Eli insisted that doing so crossed a professional boundary and yet struggled not to share parts of his life with her.

Harriet motioned for them to follow. "I have iced tea waiting."

Eli and Julia took two chairs. Will sat next to Harriet on the couch and opened his laptop. Ben hovered near the doorway.

"Ms. Wilson, do you remember the day the police were at my house?" Julia asked.

Her eyes teared up. "That was such an awful day. I'm so glad you've stopped by to see me today because I honestly didn't believe the reports that you'd survived. I mean, you didn't testify in the trial or anything."

Julia placed her elbows on her knees and leaned forward. "I'm sorry. I should have come to see you when I was all better. I've missed you."

Her nursing assessment skills kicked in. Had anyone filled the void that Julia left? The old woman had definitely lost weight—which might not have been a bad thing. There were other signs that were more disturbing to Julia. Her dove-gray hair was much longer—gathered in a braid that went all the way down to her midback. But the strands were brittle, dry. Her skin looked sallow. Julia would need to look in her refrigerator before they left to make sure she was stocked up for a while.

Ms. Wilson waved off impending tears. "I'm just so thankful to see you today. You look so happy."

Happy?

"Do you remember anything about that day?" Julia asked.

"I remember the neighbor who came by looking for cake ingredients."

Julia pressed her feet into the floor to keep her legs from shaking. "Yes, that's the man I'd like to talk to you about. We'll see if you can describe him for Will."

"It was the strangest thing. He said he lived just down the street, but I'd never seen him before. That may not mean too much. I don't like to go out."

"Tell me what happened when he stopped by," Eli asked.

"Oh my. It was so early in the morning. He got me up out of bed. It's like he had this whole list of ingredients he needed. I felt like a grocery store. He said it was his little boy's birthday and his wife didn't buy the things he needed to bake a cake. I mean, why was he baking the cake anyway?"

"What sorts of things did he ask for?" Ben asked.

Harriet began to tick things off on her fingers. "Flour. Salt. Who doesn't keep those things on hand? Shortening. Now, these days, most probably don't have Crisco on hand, but I do."

"Harriet, was there anything you didn't have on hand for this gentleman?"

"Eggs. I didn't have any eggs."

"What did he do then?" Ben asked.

Julia caught Eli's eyes. He gave her a nod. Perhaps Ben wasn't completely useless for this interview even though he didn't agree with doing it.

"At first, I just told him I didn't have any. But then he insisted I call someone to see if they did. You were the first person I could think of. Really, the only one."

Eli mouthed something to Will that Julia couldn't quite make out.

"He asked me to call you and ask for eggs."

"Me specifically?" Julia asked.

Harriet nodded. "Yes, he did use your name. I didn't find it strange if he was our neighbor."

Will positioned his laptop so Harriet could see it. "Great. What we're going to do is create a picture on my computer of what this man looks like. Let's start with his nose."

"Do you know Rock Hudson?" Harriet asked. "He had a nose just like him."

Will laughed. "Can't say I'm really familiar with him, but I'll just Google a picture and I'll find a nose that compares. While I do that, what else can you remember?"

"His eyes were the most distinctive, dark green. Seriously, just like that man over there." She turned to face Ben. "Do you have a brother?"

"I don't have any siblings," Ben said.

Will pivoted the screen toward Harriet. "How about this nose?"

She studied the image. "I don't know. It's a little off."

"Let's stick with it for now. How about the shape of the man's eyes? Round? Almond?"

"Oh, I don't know. This is so hard. I hate computers."

The green eyes that Julia remembered flashed into her vision. Now she could easily recall this most striking feature, as well. They were similar to Ben's eyes. Julia's palms began to sweat.

"How about the shape of his face?" Will asked. "Square? Triangle?"

"Now, that's where you're totally different," Harriet playfully swatted the air in Ben's direction. "The neighbor's face was definitely like a square box. Very strong chin—like John Wayne."

Julia exhaled slowly. How could she even remotely suspect Ben when he'd saved her life—on more than one occasion? The stress was causing her to become paranoid and hypersensitive.

"One John Wayne jaw coming up. Talk to me about his hair."

"Long. I never like it when men wear their hair long. Julia, what about you?"

"You're right, Harriet. Definitely short hair on a guy."

"Like Eli's. I like your hair, young man."

Eli fidgeted in his seat uneasily. "Thank you, Ms. Wilson. I don't get very many compliments on my hair."

"Well, *it is* messy. You need to comb it. Use some of that fancy hair gel to keep it in place."

Julia chuckled. She'd forgotten how funny Harriet was. Then a creeping hole snuck its way into her gut. Her assailant had taken so much from her, but he'd also taken her away from Harriet. It was time to correct that.

"Do you like Julia?" Harriet asked Eli.

To Julia's surprise, a flash of red dashed into his cheeks. "Yes, she's a very likable girl."

"No, I mean do you *like* her, because you won't stop stealing glances when she's not looking at you."

Julia smiled at Eli and he winked at her. "Well, it's my job to watch her now, so I guess that means I'm doing a good job of it."

"How about this, Ms. Wilson?" Will asked. "Does this look like the man who stopped to visit you that day?"

"It's close—"

"We can work with it, then." Will flashed the computer screen Julia's way. It looked like a mash of Rock Hudson and John Wayne.

And it didn't match any fragment of memories that Julia had of the man who attacked her.

Directly after their visit with Ms. Wilson, Eli followed Julia as she crossed the lawn to the front door of her old house. According to Julia, she was still making mortgage payments on her refurbished bungalow even though she had moved to a new house. She'd been the beneficiary of her parents' life insurance policies, a total amount unknown to Eli, but enough to maintain two properties and perhaps the money she needed for her nurse's retraining.

Eli waved to the men in the FBI CSI van. Eli had worked with one of the men, Shawn Jaeger, at Aurora police before he joined the FBI. Julia's

Realtor, Maryann, opened the lock and pushed the door open.

"I'll wait in my car until you're done and then I'll get everything locked up," Maryann said.

"Great, thanks," Julia said to the woman.

No questions from Julia about potential buyers? Likely, the attempted murder would be disclosed by the Realtor and was the nail in the coffin as to why this place couldn't sell.

Eli turned to Shawn and his partner. "I don't think we need an extensive examination. Focus on the entryway, the staircase—particularly the banister, and then directly under the main beam. We're looking for any evidence of blood splatter that could have been left by the killer."

"Got it. The previous team did look at this area, but in light of what you told me about Julia's forensic interview, I do agree a second look is warranted."

The forensic pair slipped on shoe covers and grabbed their tackle boxes of equipment, armed with a couple of flashlights.

Julia sat on the porch, and Eli hovered over her, scanning the street for any perceived threats. Ms. Wilson poked her head out one of her side windows, monitoring their activities. Probably the most excitement she'd had since the day of Julia's attack.

"Don't you think someone should go in with them?" Ben asked.

Eli shrugged. "They have their specialty. We have ours."

"Then if you think you have things covered here, I'm going to sit in the car and help Will get Harriet's photo uploaded into the system. Then Quentin can decide if he wants local media to release it."

"Do what you need to do," Eli said.

The tone of his voice caused Julia to look up at Eli.

Why am I being so short with Ben? He hasn't done anything wrong that I can prove. No member of my team has done anything wrong.

Eli rubbed at the tense muscles in his neck. The situation was beginning to wear on him. Considering how many attempts there had been on Julia's life—he wondered if they could adequately protect her from all of them.

"I don't think the computer image is going to help find my attacker," Julia said as Ben walked away.

"I know. Using the program isn't really Will's forte, but no one else was available today and he'd had an introduction to it at least."

"I'm surprised you didn't ask Ben. Isn't he a computer expert?"

Eli nodded. Was she so in tune with him that she could read his mind?

"I did ask Ben thinking the same thing, but he says he was never trained in the program." Eli shoved his hands into his pockets. Was that the true cause of his irritation? He expected things from Ben that he couldn't offer. "Regardless of the quality of the photo, we know it doesn't resemble Dr. Heller."

"The man I get glimpses of isn't him, either. Is the wrong man in jail?"

How did Julia so easily tap into Eli's biggest concern after keeping her safe—that he'd been responsible for putting an innocent man in jail?

"I still don't think it can be possible that Dr. Heller wasn't involved in some way in these crimes. His DNA is present at all the crime scenes except the most recent hanging. I'm thinking we're dealing with a team and he was part of it. The thing that's unclear is why the partner became active again."

"What's usually the reason something like that happens?" Julia asked.

Eli shrugged. "I'm not a profiler, but there's usually some sort of trigger. A marriage dissolves. Loss of a job. An anniversary of the event or death of someone. Who knows? Sometimes I feel like the motives for evil are as numerous as the stars."

The forensic team exited Julia's house.

"We did find something," Shawn said.

Eli helped Julia to a standing position. "What?"

"There were a few tiny droplets of what appeared to be dried blood on the underside of the banister. It would have been hard to find on the first go-round. It tested positive, so we grabbed a few swabs for DNA."

"Is it okay for us to go inside?" Eli asked.

"I don't have any problem with it," Shawn said. "We've got what we came for."

"Julia? Any interest?" Eli asked.

"Right now—the past might be well enough left in the past until this thing is solved and I can move forward without looking over my shoulder."

Did that mean she could see herself coming back to live here? It was a kind of forgiveness Eli wasn't sure he possessed.

"Julia, would you mind sitting in the car with Ben and Will? I need to have a private conversation with Shawn."

Julia eyed him suspiciously but reluctantly walked back to the car.

"What's up?" Shawn asked.

"What will you do with the blood sample?" Eli asked.

"Well, first we need to determine if there is adequate DNA material to provide a profile."

"If you do find a DNA profile, I need you to compare it with Heller's DNA. See if it's a match or not."

"Will do. What if it's not a match?"

"It could confirm to me that the Hangman has a partner. There's a gentleman in custody I'd like to compare it to—Ryder Dymond."

"Do you have the documents needed for us to get Ryder's DNA?"

"Not yet. Let's see what you find. How long before you could come up with an answer?" Eli asked.

"When do you need it by?"

"How fast can you do it?"

"Life-and-death matter?" Shawn asked.

"Potentially."

"I'll put a rush on it—oversee it myself, but it's still going to be a couple of days."

Eli held out his hand. "I'd appreciate any help you can give me."

What he hoped above all else was that his hunch was wrong. If Eli proved Ryder was the Hangman's partner, it would assuage his concern that a member of his team was involved.

If the DNA wasn't Ryder's or Heller's, then it opened up a whole other can of worms, and Eli would have to go to Quentin with his concerns about someone involved with Julia's case also being connected with the threat against her life.

FIFTEEN

Eli was thankful for another peaceful night, but what he hadn't shared with Julia was the fact that he wasn't sleeping in his own room as she slept in the guest room. Even though he had a third-floor apartment and a security system, the easiest access point was his front door and that was where he'd been slumming at night in a sleeping bag. He maintained this guard position until the sun came up and then hid all the evidence of his sentry point in his bedroom before Julia emerged from the guest bedroom.

He didn't want to confess to himself how much he enjoyed having Julia around, and in some ways, he wanted her case to remain unsolved—if only to continue to have these moments together. Sure, he'd had girlfriends, but no one breached the steel compartment around his heart quite the way Julia had. He began to grieve the thought of not having her in his life. What would Quentin think of him—falling for a witness under his care? Would his boss ever trust his judgment again?

Julia's door cracked open. Denim jeans. A button-up white shirt and a simple scarf decorated with butterflies. Would she ever feel comfortable enough around him to leave her scars visible?

"Ready for tea?" Eli asked.

"Of course." She settled on a bar stool.

"I scrambled some eggs. Toast, butter and jelly are waiting on the table."

"It's perfect. Thank you."

"No worries. We need to leave shortly. Ben's going to meet us at the jail to have a go at Ryder. So far he hasn't been very open with Aurora police."

Julia scooped a spoonful of eggs into her mouth and made animated chewing motions and swallowed. "You should at least let me cook."

"I should for all this one-on-one attention you're getting."

"Finally—being a protected witness is tolerable."

Eli smirked. "How'd you like to be twenty-four-seven with Ben?"

"Not my idea of fun. I think I might boycott."

"Well, we shouldn't keep the FBI agent waiting. Or Mr. Dymond for that matter."

They rode to the station together in silence. Eli was hopeful the day could bring a conclusion to the mysterious hit man case. Ryder was involved—even though criminals always professed innocence—the mere fact that Julia's hit package had his fingerprints on it meant involvement on some level.

Eli positioned Julia in the observation room as he and Ben took opposite seats across from Ryder. The lowlife seemed to be trying to live up to his name. He wore a tank top cut from a short-sleeve shirt that revealed tattoos of diamonds on each shoulder. His face was haggard with a good two days' worth of beard growth. That along with the long sideburns gave him a wild-eyed appearance.

"Mr. Dymond, thanks for agreeing to meet with us today," Ben said.

"I just want to know when I'm getting out of here."

"The more you cooperate with us, the more we'll be able to help you. First, let's talk about the hit package that was anonymously delivered to your parole officer. Who do you think gave it to him?"

"My wife. She's trying to frame me," Ryder said.

Eli leaned forward. Ryder was placing himself in the situation, though not directly. Clearly, it was a vain attempt at cover, considering that Ryder had been placed at the scene of the house explosion.

"Your wife put together this hit package on a

woman you don't know to try and frame you? That's the story you're floating out there?" Eli asked.

"I don't know why Harper does half the things she does. You know...women. I just can't read them very well."

You and me both, brother.

"Okay, let's assume that you're not involved in a murder-for-hire plot. Do you know Julia Galloway?"

"I know *of* her," Ryder confessed.

"In what capacity?" Eli asked.

Ryder tossed a glance Ben's way. Did that have any meaning? Was Eli being too intense in his questioning? If so, it seemed that Ryder viewed Ben as the good cop—as someone he could align himself with for perhaps an easier interrogation.

Ben folded his hands together. A nonthreatening pose would help Ryder buy in to Ben as someone he could trust. "Any help you can give us would be greatly appreciated. It's an innocent woman's life on the line."

"Is it?" Ryder asked.

Eli felt the tension in his hands threaten to curl his fingers into a fist. "What's that supposed to mean?" He stood from the table. Maybe it was to imbibe the whole bad cop role with all he could muster.

Ryder put his cuffed hands up. "Just settle down. I just think not everyone is so innocent.

We all have secrets that could probably get us into a heap of trouble if they were known."

"Explain to us how you know Julia," Ben said.

"Her picture is on the news like every single time they talk about the Hangman. Who doesn't know Julia Galloway? And then the droning on and on about how she's a pediatric nurse—like she doesn't deserve anything bad happening to her. Why should she get a pass when bad things happen to everyone?"

"Has there been a death in your family, Ryder?" Eli asked.

His mouth fell open. Now it was almost as if Ryder forced himself not to look at Ben for support. "I had a nephew of mine die."

"How long ago?" Eli asked.

Ryder shrugged one shoulder. "A couple of years back. I don't see what it has to do with right now."

"Your son, Miles, asked Julia if she'd ever taken care of his cousin. Was Julia involved in this child's care?"

"I couldn't say."

Eli clenched his teeth, which made his headache worsen. "Do you know Dr. Heller?"

Ryder leaned his head back and groaned. "Like the same way I know Julia. The television. Can I get out of here?"

Eli grabbed the file folder that had been sitting in front of him on the dented, scratched metal table and pulled the surveillance photos from inside. "These snapshots were taken from a security camera near Julia Galloway's house. Does this man look familiar to you?"

"Not to me."

Eli tapped the paper. "Can you see the distinctive diamond tattoo this man has on his shoulder that's very similar to yours?"

"Coincidence."

"The trouble, Mr. Dymond, is that your prints were found on the hit file. This photo places you at the scene moments before Julia Galloway's neighbor's house explodes that nearly killed a woman and her son."

Eli was amazed at how quickly the blood drained from Ryder's face. The deep black lines on his diamond tattoos appeared almost disembodied—the white color like chalk against the now pale skin.

Ryder's next phrase was even more surprising. "It's not possible."

"What's not possible?" Eli asked.

Ryder's eyes rolled so far back in his head that Eli thought he was going to pass out and then he leveled a gaze at Ben. Was he done communicating with Eli?

"Because *he* said no one would be home—that the only dead people would be Julia and a few worthless agents."

"Who said this to you?" Eli asked.

Now Ryder's gaze bored into Eli. Ironically, not

one of pure evil, but one of sadness. "The man who wants Julia Galloway dead."

And yet you were still willing to murder innocent people.

"I needed the money," Ryder confessed. "Killing Julia was a means to an end. A mutual means to an end."

Eli should have been ecstatic. What slipped from Ryder's lips was as close to an outright confession as Eli could hope for. The problem was this mysterious man was still out there and clearly a threat to Julia.

"Who is this man?" Ben asked.

Ryder's laugh sent ice through Eli's veins. Evil blossomed from a seed that was present in every human—it was the events in a person's life that determined whether or not something sprouted. The only problem was—stopping that growth once it took hold was impossible.

"All I can say is that I hope he finishes his mission." Ryder squared his eyes to the double mirror behind Eli, no doubt for Julia's benefit, and slid his finger across his throat.

Eli's blood became sludge, and a piercing pain spread through his chest. What were they up against? Could they stop the man who'd hired Ryder in time?

Julia wanted to vomit. Knowing someone existed—no, that more than one person existed whose objective in life was to see her dead made her want to head for the hills and hide in some apocalyptic bunker and not come out until the radiation from this toxic soup of revenge cleared. Eli and Ben exited the interrogation room. Ben left the observation room without even glancing her way. Eli stood against the closed door.

In his eyes was a cataclysm of fear and worry. There was no denying the attraction between them, but Ryder's declaration seemed to solidify his resolve to keep an emotional distance.

What Julia's mind begged for was Eli's embrace—to feel that protective solitude his arms afforded her that she never experienced with any other man. To have his physical closeness.

Would this danger ever end?

Eli's blue eyes circled the room and he raked his fingers through his hair. "I'm going to figure this out. Something will break."

Julia turned in the chair she sat in and rested her head on her forearms. He pulled a chair up next to her and settled a hand on her back, which only made her start to cry. How could she feel so alone and yet so close to someone? Her world was upside down. She didn't have a home. She couldn't contact her grandfather without marking him with a bull's-eye. Considering what had happened to the people around her so far, seeing him could end his life.

Having forced isolation made the losses Julia

suffered more acute. What she wouldn't give to sit in her mother's kitchen sipping fresh lemonade as her mother baked a batch of her famous chocolate chip cookies—her mother's cure for any ill that Julia suffered regardless of the time of year. To huddle into the side of her father and have him drape his arm over her shoulders—leaning in to kiss her hair.

So much of God was a mystery to her. In her mind, it made the most sense that God created the world. The intricacies of life were too much for her to believe in happenstance. And she believed that He had an active part in her life, but how much? Was it true that He controlled each and every breath? That He knew the count of the hairs on her head?

She heard a sigh escape Eli's lips. She allowed the tears to flow down her cheeks. What did it matter if he saw her cry anyway? He'd seen her at her worst—in the depths of despair, loneliness and basically in the state of a drowned rat.

"What can I do, Julia?" Eli asked.

What else could he do? He was doing everything he possibly could.

When she didn't answer, he said, "Perhaps talking to Dr. Heller will be the piece to this puzzle that we're missing."

Julia dried her eyes. She had to be stronger than this. Wallowing in self-pity wasn't going to solve anything. Somehow she had to come up with the strength she didn't feel she possessed to get through this.

Lord, I've been here before. Stuck in a hole that I can't get out of. Give me the strength I need to get through this. Help me see what I need to see to help Eli solve this crime. Keep us safe. Protect all of us—me, Eli, Ben and all who are trying to find this hit man before he hurts anyone else.

"All we can do is take the next step," Eli said. "Do you want to go with me on this interview with Dr. Heller, or should I make arrangements for another agent to come and get you?"

Separating from Eli wasn't an option.

Julia could hardly keep her thoughts straight as Eli drove to Sterling, Colorado—the only correctional facility in the state where death row inmates were held. After going through several security checks, Eli and Julia waited in the contact room for Dr. Mark Heller to be pulled from his cell, where he spent twenty-three hours a day alone. Because of the potential risk her scarf proposed, the guards insisted she remove it. Eli's gun had been checked into a locker.

The door opened, and the rattle of chains across the cement floor raced up Julia's spine like the tip of a cold knife. Dr. Heller was markedly thinner than Julia remembered. His cheeks sunken. His skin doughy and greasy. The gray hair on his head thin and shorn in a military-style crew cut. The green, jail-issued scrubs didn't improve his color.

The guards sat him in the chair on the other side of the table from Eli and Julia. Mark smiled at her, and she couldn't help returning the gesture. The Dr. Heller she remembered was nothing like the man portrayed in the media. What she recalled of their time together was a physician committed to helping children—a compassionate healer—not a murderous letch.

"Dr. Heller. My name's Eli Cayne—"

"No introductions necessary. A man doesn't forget the one who worked so tirelessly to put him behind bars—let alone ensure that he got the death penalty."

Eli had warned Julia this would happen. It was hard in jail to not make a list of enemies you wanted revenge against—even if you weren't a murderer.

"However, you did bring one of my favorite nurses with you, so perhaps I'll cooperate more than I thought I would." He reached for Julia as if to hold her hands, but his chains prevented the movement. Julia could see the guard edge forward, a warning about to spill from his lips, but Dr. Heller sighed and leaned back in his chair.

What Julia didn't feel was danger. Dr. Heller's eyes weren't the emerald green of her assailant, but hazel. Perhaps his eyes could morph into the green that her attacker possessed, but Julia was doubtful. The possible green of his chameleon eyes wouldn't be as bright and brilliant as those of the man who nearly took her life.

Then how did Heller's blood get in her house? Had he come later to help the man at the door? If so, why would he be so careless? Surely, a medical doctor was smart enough to at least deduct the most basic principle of Being a Criminal 101—do not leave your DNA behind.

"Mark, I don't know how to explain why we're here," Julia said.

Heller raised one eyebrow Eli's way. "I guess a new Hangman victim complicates your case a little bit."

Julia and Eli sat together so closely at the other side of the table that Julia could feel his muscles tense next to her. She moved to settle a calming hand on his knee but thought better of it.

Eli cleared his throat. "I understand your anger at me—particularly if you are innocent. Remember, your help in this matter could help your appeal, so I expect you to drop that tone and have a civil conversation. Otherwise there's no reason for us to carry on. I can solve this without you."

"Can you?" Heller challenged. "Because I tried several times to help you before my case went to trial and you wouldn't have anything to do with me. I guess it was hard for you, Eli, to critically look at the clues and not jump to the easy bait."

Julia placed her fingertips on the table. "The reason we're here is that someone is trying to kill me. We're trying to find out who this person is—"

"Your partner perhaps," Eli floated out.

"Since I didn't commit these crimes, I didn't have a partner."

Eli shoved his chair back, and the metal scraping against linoleum sent icy threads through Julia's body. Was Eli disengaging? Or did he feel he couldn't set aside his disdain to have a productive conversation?

"Tell me," Julia said. "What's your theory of these crimes?"

"Have you wondered why the Hangman became active again?" Heller asked.

Eli nodded but didn't say anything.

"I knew Evelyn Roush—pretty well as a matter of fact."

"In what capacity?" Eli asked, the disdain gone from his tone.

Julia's heartbeat settled down a little. Perhaps this could be a productive interaction.

"She approached me about three years ago."

"What did she want?" Julia asked.

"Her company, Medical Interventions International, developed a new style of ventilator that was able to read brain activity to know when the patient was going to take a breath. It had been successful in adults, but she wanted a research trial in pediatrics."

"What's the benefit of that for a patient?" Eli asked.

As Dr. Heller talked, Julia began to remember how excited the unit was for this type of life-support equipment. Coordinating the patient's breathing with a ventilator was hard. When the patient medically improved enough to come off the machine, he had to prove he was strong enough to breathe on his own. The best thing to progress a patient to this point was for the patient to feel as though his breathing was as natural as possible, which meant there couldn't be a lag between when a patient triggered a breath and when the machine gave one. Breathing is generated from nerve impulses originating in the brain. If a machine could sense these nerve impulses, the patient would have a more natural breathing pattern.

"That was like speaking Chinese, Doc," Eli said.

"The important thing to understand is that the technology was the most advanced thing to come along ever for ventilator support."

"What was Evelyn's proposition?"

"A multicenter research trial. Things like this take time to get approval. Clinical trials need to go through a special review board. It adds prestige to your hospital if you can be aligned with breakthrough discoveries like this one."

"You would get a benefit as well, right?" Eli asked.

"Of course. I'm not one to risk my professional career without getting some recognition in the process, but this machine really *was* good for patients. The adult studies showed that it decreased overall ventilator time, which led to a bunch of other positive benefits. The less time patients are in the hospital, the less they're exposed to life-threatening infections, and their risk for mortality decreases."

"The longer you stay in the hospital, the more at risk you are for infection and death?" Eli asked.

Heller nodded. "I merely repeat what the medical studies show."

"Were there any problems in the adult trials?" Julia asked.

He turned his attention back to Julia. "There had been a few deaths, but it was unclear if it was related to the machine or to how ill the patient was. When a hospital decides to run these trials and you are working with a population of sick people—many times it's assumed that it's the trial that caused their death, but oftentimes the illness they suffer from is just as responsible."

"How many deaths in the adult population?" Eli asked.

"None that could solely be attributed to the ventilator."

"Dr. Heller—it's not like you're at risk of losing your license or anything," Eli said.

"Three deaths in thousands of patients. Hardly significant."

Julia understood what he meant in the medical sense. There was always the weight of benefitting the patient versus causing harm, and to move medical advancement forward...there would always be patients who died as a result. It was hard for people outside medicine to understand this quandary without feeling that the medical establishment was being reckless with people's lives.

"What does all this have to do with your case and the death of Evelyn Roush?" Eli asked.

"Have you ever wondered why the Hangman is active now?"

"Why do you think?" Julia asked.

"During our trial we had two pediatric deaths. In the first death, there was no question that it was related to the patient's illness. Overwhelming sepsis. Not much to be done there."

"And the second?" Eli asked.

"Clearly related to the ventilator. Julia, do you remember this child?"

"Yes, he was around twelve. Had tried to—"

"Hang himself."

"Someone so young?" Eli said.

"We could have all sorts of discussions about

the state of society, families and teaching kids how to deal with failure, but it's not unheard of. What we don't know is if he meant to kill himself or if he was participating in some sort of game."

"What happened with the machine in this boy's case?" Eli asked.

"The breathing machine delivered successive breaths without letting any air come out. Your lungs are like balloons and they'll pop when they get overinflated. That's what happened, and he eventually succumbed to the complications from that event. The hospital was quick to pay out millions. This is what you, as in the police, never understood. Each of the Hangman's victims took care of this child."

This. One. Child. Could it be true? And if so, did Dr. Heller remember the name of the patient? Did Julia? Getting the hospital to release any records, particularly if they were related to a lawsuit, wasn't going to happen in the span of one or two days.

"We checked a similar angle—since all the victims were part of health care in some capacity, but not all the victims worked at just one hospital."

"Then you didn't check the right way," Heller said.

Julia recalled the respiratory therapist that had been part of a float agency.

Heller continued. "The Hangman's second victim, Theresa, was a nurse the hospital was hav-

ing trouble with and had been fired as a result of
inputting bad patient data that led to an overdose
of a drug. She had other problems, but that was
the biggest."

The potassium error?

"I'm not sure what the hospital would or
wouldn't have disclosed, but by the time Theresa
popped up dead she'd been employed by another
care facility for at least six months."

"I still don't understand how the CEO of MII
is the linchpin to your case," Eli said.

Heller leaned forward and licked his dry,
cracked lips, his voice low, almost as if these walls
weren't thick enough to keep the secret he was
about to divulge.

"The FDA just approved that ventilator for use
in pediatrics. Many hospitals will begin to use
it and they won't need special permission. The
Hangman is killing the people he thinks are responsible for this child's death—he's likely a rela-
tive of this boy."

"The CEO's death changed your mind?" Julia
said.

"Let's just say her death focused my vision. My
malpractice attorney had a copy of this patient's
record for review before the hospital settled. After
Evelyn's unfortunate event hit the news, I had him
review the patient's chart to see if each of these
workers was involved with this patient."

"And?"

"Every. Single. One."

"Why didn't you share this with the police?" Eli asked.

"My goal is to use this information for an appeal. What can you do? What would the DA do? He's not exactly shown his willingness to assist in overturning cases."

Eli's frown confirmed to Julia what Heller said was true.

"How do you explain your blood at the Hangman's crime scenes?" Eli asked.

"I've been thinking a lot about that, too."

He reached for Julia again and then shook his head when he couldn't touch her. "My wife, do you remember her?"

"Karen? I know who she is, but I don't think I ever worked with her."

"She worked in the directed donation section of the blood bank."

Something burst inside Julia's chest. Why would a woman betray her husband in such a way? Frame him for heinous murders?

"Let me see if I follow," Eli said. "Julia has mentioned to me that you've given blood for patients who are having surgery. Your wife would have access to your blood because she works with the units that are given for specific patients, so she's the Hangman?"

Heller shook his head. "No, I don't think she'd have the strength to do what the Hangman does."

"But what's the reason she would do something so…"

"Vile?"

"Exactly," Eli said. "To frame you for murder seems to be taking things to the extreme. An unbelievable extreme."

"I was having an affair with a nurse in the PICU. She became the first Hangman's victim. I think my wife gave a pint of my blood to whoever the Hangman is, and I became the perfect scapegoat."

Eli stood from the table. "Julia, I think we have what we need."

Dr. Heller stood as well and the guards approached him with the slow motion of wolves stalking their prey. "Julia, you know me. You have to believe that I would never do something so terrible."

Julia wanted to reach out to him—to offer him some form of human comfort. How many lives had the Hangman destroyed? It wasn't just the victims—it was also their families and other innocents along the way.

Eli shoved his hands into his pockets. "I'm going to take what you said very seriously, Dr. Heller. If you are innocent of these crimes, I promise you that there won't be anyone who will work harder than me to get you out of here."

Heller nodded. "Don't want your record to be tarnished?"

"No, I don't want to live with the guilt of knowing I've sent an innocent man to jail and didn't do anything about it. If your theory proves out, I'll help you get back on your feet. I promise. I need to know that boy's name."

"Jason Montgomery."

"Do you have his birthday? Do you know where he was born? What are his parents' names?"

"Father's name is David, and the mother's name was Carolyn."

"Was?" Julia said.

"She's no longer alive. Committed suicide shortly after her son's death."

As soon as they were through security, Eli was on his phone.

The theory Heller floated out there seemed plausible, but it also had a lot of holes, which was common with criminals trying to do everything they could to get out of jail. Eli and his team still hadn't identified who had hired Ryder Dymond to kill Julia, and Eli remained unconvinced that Heller wasn't involved. What the interview proved to Eli was that Heller had a partner and that perpetrator also needed to be identified. And that man had been the one to hire Ryder. Still, Eli was going to keep his word.

"FBI Forensics Lab. Shawn Jaeger speaking."

Eli's breath caused static on the line as he and Julia walked back to his car. "Shawn. Eli Cayne.

A slow exhalation. "Eli, I don't have anything for you yet."

"I'm calling on a different issue."

"Same case?" Shawn asked.

"Yes. Can you tell if blood left at a crime scene comes from a donated pint of blood?" Eli asked.

"We wouldn't think that right off. I don't believe I've ever had a case like that, but we'd get suspicious if the blood at the scene didn't clot or had a low DNA yield. After the person donates, the components of blood are separated into packed red blood cells, platelets and some other things, and packed red blood cells don't have the same amount of DNA that whole blood does."

"By what other ways could you tell?"

"You can test the blood for the preservative used in blood banking."

"Shawn—"

"Let me guess...another favor?"

"Can you look back at the blood samples used to identify Heller and test it for the preservative?"

"Now I'm intrigued. I'll get right on it," Shawn said.

Eli disconnected the call and dialed the next person he needed to talk to. "Q—I just met with Heller."

"And?"

"Well, he's floating out quite a theory. Of course, he denies all involvement in the crime."

"Of course."

"I need you to get some information for me from Heller's lawyer. I don't think we have enough time to work through the hospital to get what I want. I need to locate a particular patient's father. Son's name was Jason Montgomery. Father's name David."

"What am I looking for exactly?"

"A current address. I need to talk with him. Also, I need an address for Heller's wife—or ex-wife probably. Karen Heller."

"Okay—this pertains to Julia's case?"

"I hope so."

"Eli, what's going on? You've not been updating me appropriately, and I'm not on board with you protecting Julia twenty-four-seven. We all need a break or we lose focus."

What could Eli say? He didn't want to be apart from Julia. He had already lost focus. He had to see this thing through for both their sakes.

Quentin changed tactics when Eli didn't answer. "How is Julia holding up?"

They made it to Eli's vehicle. He watched as Julia got inside but delayed a few moments.

"Ryder's interview was pretty hard on Julia's psyche. It's obvious they're still coming for her."

"You can't be alone today," Quentin said. "You need backup. Has there been a fallout between you and Ben?"

Eli chewed his inner cheek. "No, sir."

"Then come by and get him. What's your plan?"

"I'm going back to talk to Ryder's wife. I have a hunch and I need to see if it plays out. If not, hopefully by then you'll have figured out how to make contact with these other two people."

There was a rustling on the phone. "Sorry, Ben's here. He thinks you're putting Julia at risk. I'm not sure I disagree with him."

Eli huffed. He was tired of fighting these battles from people on his own team.

"Ben needs to meet me at my place in the morning by eight o'clock. If he's not there, I don't think he needs to be part of Julia's case anymore."

"I'm beginning to wonder the same thing about you, Eli. If you're the best one to keep Julia safe," Quentin said.

And then he hung up without another word.

SIXTEEN

In the rearview mirror, Ben scowled at Eli. Evidently, thinking about things overnight hadn't changed Ben's opinion about talking with Harper Dymond again. Julia seemingly tried to ignore the situation by counting trees outside the passenger's window—at least he guessed that was why she tapped her leg when no music was present.

Seriously, what is Ben's deal? Does he want to solve this case or not?

Eli fumed the more Ben frowned. Whatever the reasons were for Murphy's insolence, Eli had had it, and his very next job was to speak with Quentin about sending Ben back to the FBI. Ben wasn't proactive enough and even though he'd helped to rescue Julia on two occasions, Eli couldn't help thinking he'd done it with ulterior motives.

Not the selfless attitude Eli expected him to have.

Eli parked the car in front of Harper's house. "I'll stay here," Ben said.

Eli waited for Julia to climb out of the car before he turned to Ben sitting in the backseat. "Do you have a problem?"

"No, do you?" Contention marked Ben's words.

"It just seems you want to be anywhere else but here."

"You're right," Ben said.

"Want to voice your concern?"

"Let's see—you and Julia were already here and it didn't help in any way. You're leaving the most obvious interviews up in the air—that of Heller's ex-wife and anyone from Medical Interventions International. Being here is a waste of our time. Julia's had some emotionally trying days, and you won't give her a break. She was on the road for over four hours yesterday, yet you seem to have no concern for her welfare. You took her to a maximum-security prison to visit the man who almost killed her! One of us needs to stay out here and monitor the situation in case someone sneaks up on this house. Is that enough of a list for you?"

Eli got out of the car, leaving the keys in the ignition, and slammed the door. On some level Eli had to admit that Ben was right. He shouldn't give Ben grief for stating the obvious. He was putting Julia through a lot, but he also needed her. Somewhere in that memory of hers was the key to identifying the hit man and the Hangman's partner. The recording was there—he just needed to unlock it.

Eli fingered the piece of paper taped to the side of the front door—a notice for eviction. He rapped on the screen door with Julia one step behind him, and young Miles was the one to pull it open.

He jumped up and down, clapping his hands together. "Mommy, Mommy. It's Miss Julia!"

Harper came to the door. "Agent Cayne. I sure wish you would have called."

"Sorry to interrupt your morning, but I have a few follow-up questions I need to ask you."

Harper eyed the car in the driveway and pushed Miles back behind her. "Will this take long? I just finished making breakfast. Miles doesn't like it when it's cold."

"It won't take longer than is necessary."

Harper dropped her shoulder and released the lock on the screen door. She shielded her eyes against the sun. "Who's waitin' in the car?"

"Just my partner, Ben Murphy. He's keeping an eye out on things."

She turned to Miles. "Son, go up to your room and play some video games."

"Uncle—"

"Right now," Harper all but screamed, cutting his statement off at the knees.

Uncle?

Eli ruminated over the word. Did it have any meaning? Julia raised a puzzled eyebrow, as well.

"But why can't I stay here or play outside?" he whined.

"Just do as I say!"

Eli bristled and Julia clenched her hands at her sides. Neither of them liked children being chastised with such force undeservedly.

"He's fine," Julia said. "We really don't mind if he's here."

"Nonsense," Harper said. "The ol' saying that children are to be seen and not heard has some value. Now, Miles, do as I say."

The boy scurried up the stairs, the look in his eyes as droopy as a basset hound's. Julia wandered near the decrepit mantel, taking in the photos that sat there. Photos that hadn't been there on their first visit.

"Harper, I'm sure you're aware your husband is in custody," Eli said.

"And he'll be stayin' there. No way I can bond him out."

Couldn't or wouldn't bail him out?

"One thing that has always confused me is who dropped off the hit package to Ryder's parole officer."

Harper chewed her nails, taking a seat on the threadbare, Kool-Aid–stained love seat.

"I should thank you," Eli said. "For doing my job for me."

"How do you figure that?" Harper asked—her voice a pitch higher.

Julia stopped her browsing and turned to face the two of them.

"You're the one who delivered the hit file to Ryder's parole officer. Once you found out what Ryder was involved in, you wanted to save Julia. You probably assumed Ryder wouldn't be so stupid as to leave his prints all over it. But since they are present, it diminishes his ability for plausible deniability."

"Look, mister, Ryder has made his bed and now he has to lie in it. I just want Miles and me to be free of him. I don't want what's left of our family to be caught in his shenanigans no matter how much money we're..."

Eli let her wallow in the mud of her confession for a few moments. "Can't say that I blame you." He could see Miles tiptoeing down the stairs.

Julia snagged a photo from the mantel and pulled it close to her face. With the other hand, she gripped the edge of the fireplace.

What did she see in that picture?

Eli kept Julia in his peripheral vision as he directed his comment to Harper. "On our last visit you mentioned you'd seen too much death. Do you know a boy by the name of Jason Montgomery?"

Harper grabbed the edge of the couch with both of her hands and leaned forward as if she was going to topple over—a soft mewing escaped her lips. Julia turned the picture Eli's way—pointing to a photograph of two young boys. It was a large eight-by-ten. The youngsters each held a fishing pole and a string of fish between them. Julia tapped her finger against one of the boy's heads and mouthed *Jason*.

All of a sudden, missing puzzle pieces snapped into place for Eli. Jason Montgomery had to be related to Miles and therefore related to Ryder. That bolstered credibility for a personal vendetta as a motive for the Hangman—taking out those who had cared for this boy and didn't prevent his death.

It meant Heller could be telling the truth.

Eli didn't believe Ryder had enough intelligence to be the head of the snake. A competent partner—even that seemed to be a stretch.

A knot formed at the base of Eli's throat. It meant...the Hangman was free. What he needed most at that time was to have Julia near him—to wrap protective arms around her to keep her from the coming danger.

But from which direction was the threat coming?

"Both of you need to leave," Harper demanded.

Miles parked himself in front of the screen door. His head swiveled from side to side like that of a watchdog guarding the perimeter.

"Right now," Harper seethed. "Get out of my house. I don't want you here anymore!"

Julia set the photo back on the mantel and walked to the door. Were puzzle pieces falling into place for her, as well? Or did she just want out? The tension too much for her? Then again, ER nurses functioned under a mountain of stress every day. Miles blocked Julia's exit from the house.

"Harper, please," Eli said. If he didn't clear this up now, he wouldn't be convinced he could ward off the coming onslaught against Julia. "How is Jason related to you? I know that Julia took care of him in the hospital. That he died as a result of an equipment failure. Do you and Ryder know Jason? Is that why he's participating in this murder-for-hire plot against Julia?"

Miles shot out the door, and the screen door slammed like a bullet from a gun. Now Julia hovered there with her pediatric nurse's eyes watching over his safety, since Harper seemed unconcerned about his egress from the house.

Harper stood from the couch. "Do I have to call the police? Get out of my house!"

Julia exited, calling Miles's name.

"Miles—come back here!" It was clear that Harper wasn't in any position to keep an eye on her charge, and Julia knew a child's unmonitored exuberance was usually a ticket for admission to the ER.

The boy pumped his legs to their car where Ben sat and pounded on the window. When Ben didn't immediately respond, the boy grabbed the handle and pulled the door open, and something tumbled to the driveway.

Julia narrowed the distance and found Miles yanking items out of what appeared to be Ben's wallet. Credit cards. A driver's license. Several photos.

"Miles, give it back to me," Ben ordered.

Ben knew Miles? Julia's heart fell into her hands as she gathered the faded photographs Miles carelessly let fall onto the driveway. Ben and Jason together. Julia plucked them from the cement more quickly. Ben hugging Jason. Ben with Jason at a five-year birthday party.

"Uncle Ben! Uncle Ben! When is Cousin Jason visiting from heaven? You said I would see him again someday. Please, please—can today be the day?"

The strength in Julia's hands left her, and the pictures fluttered to the ground. Without standing, she looked up. Ben towered over her. "Miles, you won't see Jason today, but I think Miss Julia will be able to say hi for you."

Julia's heart thundered in her chest, her body frozen as she riffled through the options her mind presented to her.

"Will you do that for me, Julia?" Ben asked.

Julia reached up and placed a protective hand on Miles's shoulder.

Ben is Jason's father—or stepfather, since their last names are different, but he's the one seeking vengeance on behalf of this child. Ben Murphy is the Hangman!

Eli walked through the front door and headed for the car. It was clear Harper had closed down answering any more questions. His phone buzzed in his pocket. He grabbed it and stopped in the middle of the lawn. Julia was picking something up from the driveway—Ben hovered over her.

"Miles! Come here right now!"

Julia lifted her face to Harper but kept a firm hand on Miles's shoulder as if to keep him from leaving her side.

"Cayne," Eli snapped into his phone.

"Eli, it's Shawn Jaeger from FBI Forensics. I'm calling in regards to your request to have me test the blood found in the Hangman's case for the special preservative used in donated blood to keep it from clotting."

"And?"

"The blood that has Heller's DNA is definitely from a donated pint of blood—likely whole blood, which is why the DNA yield was so high."

Eli's heart jumped into his throat.

Shawn continued. "Your request raised several issues for our lab, as this information puts into serious question whether or not Dr. Mark Heller could have been present for any of these crimes, and so I initiated an internal investigation."

"Have there been any conclusions?" Somehow the words still came through Eli's constricted throat.

"It appears one of our own agents, Ben Murphy, paid a lab technician a good sum of money to alter the report and stand by it in a court of law."

Eli swallowed hard. "Shawn, do you know if Ben ever lost a child?"

"I do…his stepson, Jason Montgomery. He was completely devastated."

Ben and Eli locked eyes and at that moment—an understanding of their roles clarified in a nanosecond. No longer partners in the fight against evil, but lawman against criminal with the hunter's prey within his grasp.

Was there any other easier person to suspect as a hit man than someone who had a criminal background and was also having a financial crisis? When Miles said the word *uncle*, he was signifying Ben's relationship to himself. The picture of the two boys together—they were cousins. That made Ryder Jason's uncle. Add that to a financial crisis, like losing a house, someone who had a personal vendetta against a health-care team for a child's death and it was the perfect mixture of morality lost and evil filling the vacuum.

Ryder wasn't the only one trying to take Julia's life. A witness only identified him near Julia's neighbor's house.

Ben had tried to kill Julia, as well—his saving

her life a ruse to keep Eli and his team from discovering his true intentions.

The first morning Eli met Julia, Ben had not been on the doorstep clearly to stay out of the line of fire. Ben's foot pursuit a cover for his involvement. The carbon monoxide poisoning—would evidence place him as the one who'd tampered with the furnace? The remote control of Eli's car—and Ben's computer expertise.

How could I miss this? Everything was right there before me. And he's not a partner... Ben is the Hangman.

Ben shoved Miles to the ground and advanced on Julia—unholstering his gun. Julia's hands drifted up in the air as she looked back at Eli.

Ben grappled Julia around the upper body, lifted her up and backpedaled her to the front passenger's side of their car—rounding it more quickly than Eli thought possible.

Eli drew his weapon, but with the way Ben's head bobbed back and forth behind Julia's, he couldn't get a clear shot. The front end of the car providing additional cover.

"Ben! Stop right now. Killing Julia isn't going to accomplish anything. Let her go!"

"This is for my son. This is for Jason!"

Ben aimed his weapon at Eli and fired off a round. Eli ran toward Miles, who had crawled away from the car but was positioned between the house and the driveway, and tackled him into the grass, covering the boy's body with his own.

Ben continued to fire shots, a startled scream tingling Eli's ears as he anticipated the iron-hot spindle of pain hitting his own body at any moment. His heart hammered in his ears—almost as loud as the gunfire. He covered Miles's head with his hands and turned to see Harper lying on the front porch, her hands holding her belly.

The car door slammed. Eli looked back to see Ben rounding the front end of the car and scurrying inside. The engine turned over, and Ben threw the car in Reverse.

Eli couldn't believe leaving the keys in the car for Ben's comfort had just aided the escape of a madman.

Eli stood up and aimed his gun at the car as it reversed down the driveway. Julia heeded his earlier warning, as he couldn't see her sitting upright on the passenger's side. That or Ben held her head down. For what purpose? What was the point in keeping her alive for the moment when he'd hired Ryder to kill her?

Eli squared his stance and fired a couple of shots at the windshield—hoping against hope the flying metal would hit its mark. The windshield starred, but the car continued to move backward. Eli ran after it. As the car slowed slightly as Ben put the car in Forward, Eli fired his remaining rounds at the tires. Nothing took.

Eli raced back to the house and approached Harper. Miles cried as he kneeled next to her in the grass. She was cringing, rolling side to side as blood pooled from the wound in her abdomen. Eli removed his suit coat and rolled up one sleeve.

"This is going to hurt." Eli pressed the bundle into her abdomen and then spoke into his wrist mic. "Shots fired. Shots fired."

His heart pounded in his chest. The next words were ones he didn't want to speak. "Agent Murphy has taken Julia Galloway hostage."

"Copy that." The dispatcher sounded distant.

"I need a rescue unit and…everyone. He's in a late-model…"

"We've got the car's make and model. We'll get a BOLO to local PD."

Once he knew help was on the way, he placed his free hand behind Harper's head and lifted it gently off the ground. "Harper, where would Ben take Julia?"

She clenched her eyes closed and moaned.

"Please, Harper, if you don't want to go jail, then you have to tell me right now where Ben might go."

Her eyes flared open, wide and glassy, as the blood oozed from beneath Eli's sleeve into the grass. "I don't know, but take my car. Ryder knows where Ben would go."

What could he do? Leave Harper here to bleed out? Leave her with her son providing her care and then she dies anyway and the boy lives with the guilt of his mother dying at his hands?

Neither option was viable.

He'd have to wait for the ambulance. Eli buried his face into the crook of his arm and did the last thing he could do on Julia's behalf until Harper was safe.

Lord, protect her. Help me find her before it's too late.

SEVENTEEN

The gunshots stopped, and Julia raised her head from the seat. Ben drove with his head shifted to the left because of the starburst caused from Eli's bullet hitting the windshield. As Julia braced her hands against the top of the seat, shards of safety glass felt like rocks under her palms. Looking at Ben, she could see a circular mark of blood under his left arm.

Evidently, Eli was a good marksman.

"Pull over, and I'll help you," Julia said.

"Above all things, I don't need your help. You've *helped* my family enough."

What would Eli do? Could he save her? She knew he could, but would he figure out this last remaining piece of the puzzle? Where was Ben taking her? What was the last part of his plan?

He switched to steer with this right hand and braced his gun low against his abdomen with his left and pointed it at her side. Even though he was bleeding, Julia guessed at best it was a grazing shot. The bleeding wasn't brisk enough to be anything serious, and Ben's adrenaline was better than any dose of morphine she could have given him.

They stopped at a light, and a police officer pulled up next to them but had his face turned the other way typing at his computer.

Julia's heart thumped wildly in her neck. Would he see it—the starred windshield that obstructed Ben's view? That had to be reason enough to pull him over.

"Don't think about signaling that officer. If you do, I'll not only kill you, but I'll kill him, too. And who's he going to believe anyway—an FBI agent or some crazy woman he's bringing into custody who wrestled his weapon free at one point and shot through his windshield?"

Julia decided it best not to argue the illogical scenario he proposed. Why would the officer believe him when she wasn't in handcuffs? Then again, why give Ben any more thoughts on how to detain her? Right now, with her arms and legs free, escape was possible if she could find the right opportunity.

The light turned green and the police officer turned right without so much as glancing their way.

Julia folded her hands in her lap and began to pray but kept her eyes on the road before them.

Lord, I don't see any way out of this without

someone dying. I pray that You be with Eli—keep him safe and help him to find me before it's too late. Whatever has caused this vengeance in Ben, let me be able to break through it. I know he can love if he loved his son so much that he's willing to kill other people because the loss was so great for him.

"What did I do? What did any of us do to deserve death?" Julia's heart told her not to challenge him. What was the wisdom in antagonizing him? ER nurses were used to asking pertinent questions but not always at the right time.

"You didn't stop it when you could have."

Stop what? The more she thought about it, the more she remembered Jason Montgomery's case. The patient's history stated he'd been found by his stepfather, hence the different last names, hanging by a belt in his closet. Trouble had followed Jason like a shadow he couldn't shake. Depression. Oppositional defiant disorder. The psychiatric team theorized it stemmed from his unresolved conflict surrounding his parent's divorce.

Jason also exhibited a high level of risk-taking behavior—coming home drunk and high on marijuana. So the trouble with the nature of his injury was no one really knew if it was accidental or intentional.

"What did you want me to stop?" Julia asked.

It was one of those rare times she could say and ask a parent whatever she wanted to, because if her death was as imminent as Ben insinuated, then she might as well know the truth.

"You and your coworkers were talking about the ventilator. How another kid had died and *you* let them use it on my son. Your job was to speak up for him when no one else would."

Julia exhaled slowly, trying to ease the growing ball of anxiety in her belly. It was a common problem in health care—a parent overhearing unit gossip and not understanding what was true and what wasn't. What was just blowing off steam and what was the hallmark black humor they used to deal with stress.

She didn't excuse it—she wasn't perfect.

In the previous patient case Ben mentioned, it wasn't clear to the nursing staff if the newfangled machine was at fault, but there was worry among the staff about the possibility. Doctors assured them that one death did not a suspicious series make.

"I'm sorry. I don't know what else to say."

Ben turned off the road and angled his car into a wooded area. Julia's body felt numb. Was this it? He would just shoot her dead among the trees and leave her body for scavengers? And then what would he do? Did he imagine that he'd be able to escape his way out of this?

"Why don't I remember meeting you?" Julia asked.

"Because we never met. You worked days and

I visited at night after work, but the one conversation I overheard happened at shift change—so many of you felt the same thing and never spoke up. You failed Jason."

He positioned the car to the side of the dirt road, threw his door open, ran around to her side of the car and then pulled hers open. "Get out."

She complied, keeping her hands visible.

And then he threw a gun to her feet. Her gun. So he'd taken it. "Pick it up."

It seemed counterintuitive that he would give her something she could defend herself with. What kind of sick game was he playing?

She picked it up but kept it at her side pointed to the ground.

"Do you know what my plan is?" he asked with a maniacal lilt to his voice.

Sweat tricked down the side of her face. "I don't."

"I'm going to go to the hospital where Jason died and kill as many people as I can. You'll be among them."

Julia ran the tip of her tongue over her dry lips while she contemplated her options. Breathing slowly, she tried to stem the riptide of adrenaline that threatened to fuzz her thinking. Should she scream for help? Who would hear her? Take the gun and try to get a shot off before Ben shot her? She was anything but a sure shot. In the gun, she only kept one bullet. Her plan was always to fire a warning shot to scare off an intruder, but if the intruder got the weapon away from her...there wouldn't be any more bullets to use against her. Julia hadn't practiced with the weapon as often as she should have for a situation like this. In her heart, she knew she would never be capable of intentionally taking someone's life.

Now she reweighed that credo.

"Or?" Julia asked.

"You think there's another option?"

"Why else would you bring me here?"

Ben smiled. "Julia Galloway. No matter what I think of you..." He laughed to himself. "I really like you. You're smart. Funny. I can see why Eli's been pining for you."

Had she heard him right? Sadly, it wasn't appropriate to pump your captor for information about whether or not somebody had an attraction. Particularly when it was clear he wouldn't be satisfied until she was permanently encased in a crypt. What it did tell her was that Eli had feelings for her and wouldn't give up looking for her. She had to stay alive long enough for that to happen. That was her job.

"I like you, too," Julia offered. How would this play out?

He folded his arms over his chest but kept the gun aimed her way. "That actually sounded sincere."

"It was. I know the pain of losing loved ones.

I've had pain in my life like that, too." *Because if you hadn't nearly killed me, my parents wouldn't have died in that car accident.* "I know you loved Jason with everything in you for you to go to these lengths and do these things. You can begin to heal from that pain right now by not hurting anyone else. You can stop this path you're on. If you kill me, you'll never have a moment of peace again."

Ben opened his arms wide. "Who says I want peace? Do you know what it's like to live in this deep, dark pit that you can't climb out of? Even though Jason wasn't my biological child, that boy meant everything to me. My only chance at fatherhood."

"You don't have an out? You plan on dying at the hospital, as well?"

"That, Julia, is true. I have contingencies for a lot of things except the scenario I'm going to present to you. That's how you ensure my death— deny the choice that I'm about to give you."

"Which is?"

He aimed his gun back at her chest. "Take that gun and kill yourself. If you do, you have my sincere promise that I won't drag you back to that place you call a center of healing, bring you to the PICU, to the room where Jason died, and kill as many people as I can until they kill me."

Her hand sweated so badly that the gun almost slipped from her fingers. His proposal sent an arrow of fear straight through her heart. Was she willing to do as he asked to save others? In truth, she couldn't trust him to do as he said—which was annihilating every person who took care of his child.

Innocent people.

"Mark Heller is innocent, isn't he?"

"I guess it depends on how you qualify that word."

"Meaning he didn't kill anybody."

"That is true—he didn't kill anybody in the physical sense, but his actions did end his marriage. I guess you could call that a death of sorts."

"How did you do it—set him up for the murders?"

In Julia's mind, there were several reasons why Ben brought her here—the one he presented probably being the last on his list. There was something about confession that was freeing. Although Ben might not consciously realize it, he wanted to get what he'd done off his chest—all his misdeeds. And what better way to do that than with someone who wouldn't be around to spill the secrets?

"Sometimes perfect things happen through serendipity." He shifted his stance. "I got to know a phlebotomist named Karen who came to Jason's bedside on occasion to do specialized blood tests. Some people can't help oversharing. It's a defect, I would say—particularly when you're in a professional capacity.

"I found out many things from Karen. How she

was married to the great Dr. Heller...and that the man everyone fell to their knees for was hardly one to be idolized. He cheated on her and she actually pointed to one of the nurses who was caring for Jason as the woman he strayed with."

"What does this have to do with you framing Dr. Heller for these murders?"

"Karen and I bumped into each other at a coffee shop shortly after Jason's death. She offered the usual condolences, but then the conversation turned in an unexpected way. I couldn't stop thinking about those people who didn't express their concerns about the ventilator and its potential to take a life instead of sustain it and how I wanted them to pay."

"And Karen's problem?"

"Simple...if it ever is—hatred for her husband and his womanizing ways. One thing led to another and she offered to give me a pint of his blood if I would do just one thing—make it look like he killed his mistress. Then she could have access to all his money while he wasted away in prison."

A clammy sweat bubbled on Julia's skin. It amazed her how easy it was for some people to tap into evil.

"This nurse cared for Jason. I realized we could both have what we wanted, and Dr. Heller could die with a needle in his arm. It was...perfection. And there would be enough of his DNA to spread the wealth around as they say."

"But the police linked the cases too quickly."

"Sadly, yes. This I have to take responsibility for. I was too anxious to do as the wife asked and killed the mistress first when I should have saved her for last. Heller's DNA was found all over her apartment, which caused them to type it against the blood on the rope, and since my crime scenes were unique, they naturally thought to compare all the DNA. It was a good thing for me that the DNA testing got delayed because another crime took precedence over mine, which allowed me to kill most of the people on my list."

"Why did you start killing again?"

"The ventilator that killed my son was going to be used on other children and I couldn't let that happen. I figured Evelyn Roush deserved the Hangman's death and I could try to make it look like a suicide to keep the police off my trail. A hit man was the best choice for you to make it appear like the same person wasn't back to finish you off and Heller could continue to rot in jail. Who knew my relatives would be so incompetent and morally minded—even with a criminal history? I had to take matters into my own hands when Harper delivered the hit file to Ryder's parole officer. The explosion was the only thing Ryder accomplished but ended up not achieving the end goal. I thought for sure blowing up that house would take you out but spare my own life and the damage would destroy any evidence contained in your book of confession—that pesky journal you found."

"All people have a capacity for change. It's still possible for you, too."

"I don't have any desire to change this course. Now, Julia, it's time for you to choose. What will it be? Your death at your own hand to save many? Or your death at my hand and many more die?"

"I'll only do it if you clear Mark Heller's name."

Did the lie sound as convincing as she wanted it to?

The smirk on Ben's face solidified in Julia's heart the action she had to take. "No deal."

She brought her weapon up and aimed straight for his chest and fired.

Eli grabbed Ryder by the shirt and pummeled him into the wall. Every muscle fiber in his body burned to do whatever damage was necessary to pull the information needed from Ryder to save Julia's life.

"Tell me where your brother-in-law is going with Julia," Eli seethed, remnants of his words spraying Ryder in the face.

It was the first time in his career that he'd used physical force to try and scare an individual, and it sent an unknown dismay through his body. Not that he thought himself beyond physical force— no, it proved to Eli how desperate he was to save

Julia. And desperation like that only stemmed from fear of losing some that you…

Loved.

Seeing Julia disappear with Ben sent his mind reeling. Imagining that they would never be together wasn't acceptable. It was so much more than saving a witness—it was saving the one he was meant to be with forever.

He shoved hard again. "Tell me!"

Will and Jace pulled them apart and tossed Ryder into a chair.

Eli shoved a finger centimeters from Ryder's face. "You don't get it. If she dies, so much more is going to happen to you. You're going to be brought up on charges for arson—perhaps even using a weapon of mass destruction, considering that you built a pipe bomb. Next is assault and battery for injuring the mother and son in the explosion. Conspiracy to commit murder. With all these things, you'll never get out of jail, but if you want to avoid the death penalty you better help me save Julia before Ben kills her."

"Who would believe the federal agent who put an innocent man away?"

Eli brought his fist high and before he could smash it into Ryder's face, he forced it into the wall. The desire to throw chairs, break Ryder's face…pull his gun and discharge it into the man's chest became more than his inhibition and he stormed from the room and escorted Miles inside.

Ryder looked away, but his chest heaved with sudden emotion.

Eli bent down and tried to present the most calm, serene face he could muster. "Miles, did you do what I asked?"

The blond-haired boy nodded and held out the picture.

"Take it to your dad. I know he misses you."

The wisdom of this maneuver was yet to be determined. It was risky. It wasn't clear what kind of relationship Miles and Ryder had. Eli could only guess Ryder loved his son with everything in him to go along with Ben's revenge plot over the loss of his nephew.

Eli stood and placed a steady hand on Miles's back and eased him forward. At first, Ryder did everything he could to not look at his son, but after a few tentative steps Miles raced to his father and wrapped his arms around his chest.

"Daddy, please...do whatever it takes to come home. I miss you."

Ryder bent his head, tears streaming down his face, and he pressed his lips into Miles's mussed-up hair.

Eli tried not to count the minutes. He tried to convince himself his silence would bring a confession from Ryder's lips. It might be the lowest play Eli had ever manipulated, but it was also a chance for Ryder to understand he didn't have to throw his life away for the sake of Ben's revenge.

"I will, Miles. I promise."

Miles set his picture on the scratched table, two crayoned stick figures holding hands by a swing set—Miles and his father and what he hoped them to be. Jace then escorted Miles from the room.

Ryder wiped his nose with the back of his handcuffed hands and looked at Eli. "He's taking her to the hospital. He wants to kill her there."

EIGHTEEN

Julia's bullet hadn't met its mark and now Ben raced to the hospital, his gun still trained on her. It was as if Julia wasn't a part of herself anymore. The events seemed separate from physical reality. If she allowed herself to sit in the passenger's seat next to Ben...she would feel the awful spindles of shock firing through her body. If she were here—above it—she could think rationally just like when a code happened.

Except that her own life was on the line.

Ben screeched to a halt near the front of the hospital and slammed the car into park. The seat belt bit into Julia skin, her hands floating appendages as the car's safety mechanism prevented her from crashing through the already injured windshield.

He exited the driver's side and left the door open. Julia punched out of her seat belt, locked the passenger-side door and began to crawl over the seats to exit the driver's side. Loud pops filled the air, echoed by screams of women and children. Glass hailed over Julia's legs and she felt a hand clamp down on her calf. Flipping onto her back, she delivered a swift kick into Ben's gut, which loosened his grip, and she continued to crawl backward out of the car. Quicker than she thought possible, he opened the passenger-side door and grabbed both her legs, yanking her out where she landed on her back on the black, oily pavement.

"Get up!"

Julia scrambled up and Ben advanced on her. She backed up into the car and he grabbed the front of her shirt, forcing her body against his and placing the gun to her temple.

"Ben, let her go!"

Eli's voice. Ben twirled Julia and grabbed her around the chest, pinning her arms with his. He began to walk her to the hospital entrance.

Julia squinted her eyes against the sun. Where was Eli? That was when she saw several other officers dressed in navy blue dotted around the front of the campus. Somehow they had discovered Ben's plot and had been there to preempt him.

Policemen beckoned patients and their families away from the hospital entrance. The screaming—why couldn't it stop? It made it hard for Julia to keep a clear head. She felt the metal end of the gun warming from the heat in her skin. She had both hands clamped on Ben's forearm to try and steady the sway of her body against his.

Ben raised the weapon and fired two shots into the air. Radios squawked in rapid succession and Julia's heart anchored at the base of her throat, beating as quickly as Ben's to her back.

"Back off!" Ben yelled, tugging her closer to the hospital entrance.

Eli revealed himself, and Julia focused her vision at his eyes and he engaged hers.

Would this be her last sight of him?

Eli held Julia's gaze. Even though she had a gun held to her head, he didn't see fear there. Just certainty. Determination.

He held two fingers up and pointed at his eyes. *Look here, Julia. Stay with me. I will get you through this in one piece.*

To his relief, Julia appeared uninjured. It looked as though one of his bullets found its mark, as blood dotted Ben's left suit sleeve, but it was apparently not enough to dissuade this man from his ultimate plan.

Once Julia's eyes held his, he straightened his stance and leveled the weapon at Ben's head. "Ben, please. I don't want to shoot you. Just surrender yourself."

Ben continued to pull Julia to the front entrance. Two uniformed officers held positions at either side of the door, their weapons trained on

Ben, as well. They couldn't shoot him in the back without fear of the bullet passing through to Julia.

Ben wasn't going to win. They weren't going to allow him to enter the hospital. The next goal was keeping Julia alive, but Eli knew some of the other officers—and even the command structure—were willing to injure Julia if it came down to preventing Ben from taking his weapon inside.

The sun beat down on the lawn, its glare bouncing off windshields. Sweat dripped into Eli's eyes. His hands ached from holding his gun.

In Ben's eyes he saw just as much determination as in Julia's. Except Ben's were filled with anger, hatred—matted pools of hopelessness that made any man an unpredictable weapon. Even without a gun.

How could Eli end this? Ben continued to take steps toward the hospital.

"Eli," Julia called. "I'm sad you never picked me flowers."

He wiped the sweat from his brow. A message for sure. He blinked rapidly to clear his vision.

"Shut up," Ben said. "Don't talk to him."

Ben and Julia were at best twenty steps from the front entrance. Eli moved closer to Ben. Now Eli was shielded under the valet parking overhang, which made it easier for Eli to find his mark.

"You know what my favorites are?" Julia asked.

Ben continued to step back, closing the distance. Eli waved the officers off. He knew what she was going to do. She was waiting for him to be prepared.

Their signal. The precious secret between them from the day they were brought back together. Daisies. Red daisies. They might not be her favorite, but they were going to be today.

Eli advanced three steps, squared up again and aimed his weapon right at Ben's head.

"Red daisies," Eli said.

Julia dropped like a weight from Ben's arms, and Eli fired his shot—finding his mark in the middle of Ben's forehead.

Keeping his gun trained on Ben, he ran toward the two of them, kicking Ben's weapon out of the way. Other officers converged on Eli's position to check Ben and to determine whether or not he was still alive. It was clear to Eli that his partner wasn't.

Eli kneeled down and gathered Julia in his arms, desperate to have her close to him. At this point, he didn't care what others thought. He didn't care if he was fired.

He was never letting her go again.

Eli pulled her up and walked her away from Ben's bloody body to a small park nearby and positioned her under the shade of a large tree. She leaned against the trunk.

He wanted to remember every bit of this moment. The smoky brown color of her eyes. The quirky smile. The curl of her blond hair and how soft and gentle it felt against his skin. He traced the contour of her lips with his finger and then his hands settled against the curve of her hips.

She reached up and raked her fingers through his hair. "Now…we're even." Her voice was faint and breathless.

Eli clasped her face in his hands. He couldn't mess this moment up like he did the last time. He searched her eyes for any hint that she didn't want this, but all he saw was sweet permission.

His lips found hers and they melted together in perfect oneness. His hands fell from her face and reached around her, pulling her tight against him. She was the one thing he'd been missing. The one thing he would never give up again.

Easing her back, he cupped the back of her neck and laid gentle kisses on her healed scars.

"Julia Galloway, I'm in love with you. Please, don't ever forget that."

EPILOGUE

Eighteen months later

Julia loved Christmas and it was a perfect day. Colorado had been gifted with a light blanket of freshly fallen crystals to put everyone in a peaceful, wintery mood. Poinsettias full of red blooms were in nearly every crevice, and the soft light of candles completed the ambience. The scent of hot apple cider filled her home.

Julia twirled her wedding ring, wanting to imprint this moment in her mind.

Her old home was now their new home.

Even though tragedy once made her flee from what she and her parents had worked so hard to perfect, it seemed natural for her and Eli to start their lives together in this place. To replace loss with new life. To live where he'd saved her. Where she'd triumphed over death.

Eli turned the television off. "Mark Heller's finally a free man."

The wheels of justice weren't known to move swiftly, but they did turn. Eli had worked tirelessly to help Heller's appeal and get him released from jail by leading a new investigation in conjunction with Aurora police to prove Ben was the Hangman. Ryder surprised everyone by pleading guilty and was currently serving jail time. Harper and Miles moved out of the area.

Julia's grandfather clapped his hands. "That's quite a gift that God gave him."

"It's quite a gift that God gave me," Eli said. He still found it hard to forgive himself for Heller's captivity and he'd continue to do what he could to make sure Heller got back on his feet.

"Is it time for presents?" Julia asked.

Her grandfather raised his empty coffee mug. "Not before I get some more of your wonderful cinnamon apple cider."

"You're not stowing jugs of this away in your room, are you?" Julia asked.

He placed a hand to his chest. "Why would I do that?"

Eli amazed her. He'd insisted on her grandfather living with them. The house had plenty of room and Eli seemed determined to nurture the family closeness he'd never known.

"Because I found a jug up there just last night," Eli said.

"You were nosing around my room?" her papa asked, laughing.

"I might have been snooping for presents," Eli confessed. "I can't help it. It's in my genes to find lost things."

"So it is." Julia smiled. "But you missed this." She pulled a present from under the tree.

"What is it?" Eli asked as she handed it to him.

"Just a little something from your wife."

"Julia…" He held her gaze, the love in his eyes bringing happy tears to hers.

Then Eli set the gift box down and settled his hands gently on her belly, blooming with his child. "This," he whispered, "is the only gift I needed."

Julia laid her hands over Eli's, and their baby girl moved as if responding to their embrace. Her husband was right—there wasn't a greater gift. Or a more beautiful promise of a new beginning.

Thank You, Lord. These things I will never forget.

* * * * *

*If you enjoyed FRACTURED MEMORY,
look for FORGOTTEN MEMORIES
by Laura Scott and
SUDDEN RECALL by Lisa Phillips
from Love Inspired Suspense.*

Dear Reader,

Imagine being home early in the morning and having a law enforcement officer knock on your door and tell you someone wanted to kill you and you needed to leave your home immediately for your own safety. Imagine the upheaval. The uncertainty. The amount of trust you'd have to put in a person you didn't even know.

My novels are inspired from snippets of real life events. This opening scenario may sound familiar to you as this is exactly what happened to one particular woman. When I saw her story, I knew I had to write a novel with a beginning like that. What I needed was a more twisted and intriguing story line with a dash of medical mystery—my own suspenseful recipe.

I became part of the Love Inspired family via the Blurb to Book contest that Love Inspired sponsored in 2014. To see the fingerprints of how God led me to participate in this contest still amazes me. It was a leap of faith for me. Writing a novel with a strong romance thread was outside my comfort zone as my previous novels were more straight thrillers. I think those feelings I had about the contest came through in how Julia Galloway has to do many of these same things as she and Eli Cayne hunt to find who is trying to kill her.

Julia has to trust a process she's unfamiliar with. She has to lean on God in moments of uncertainty.

Knowing that the contest deadlines were pretty tight, I definitely had to write a character I knew pretty well. Julia's nursing career basically mimics my own. I did start in adult nursing and lasted about three years before I decided that pediatric nursing was truly where my heart was. Also, my novels usually have some sort of medical twist, and I'll be interested to hear from Love Inspired readers what they think of my debut novel with this line.

I've been welcomed so warmly into the Love Inspired family by the editorial staff and my fellow authors, and I'm very excited to get to know readers, as well. Please email me with your thoughts on *Fractured Memory* at jredwood1@gmail.com, or write to me at Jordyn Redwood, PO Box 1142, Parker, CO 80134.

Many blessings,
Jordyn

LARGER-PRINT BOOKS!

GET 2 FREE LARGER-PRINT NOVELS PLUS 2 FREE MYSTERY GIFTS

Love Inspired®

Larger-print novels are now available...

LILP15

REQUEST YOUR FREE BOOKS!
2 FREE WHOLESOME ROMANCE NOVELS
IN LARGER PRINT
PLUS 2
FREE
MYSTERY GIFTS

✽✽✽✽✽✽✽✽✽✽✽✽✽✽✽✽✽✽✽✽✽✽✽✽✽✽

HEARTWARMING™
❦❦❦❦❦❦❦❦❦❦❦❦❦❦❦❦❦❦❦❦❦❦❦❦❦❦

Wholesome, tender romances

WESTERN WP PROMISES

YES! Please send me **The Western Promises Collection** in Larger Print. This collection begins with 3 FREE books and 2 FREE gifts (gifts valued at approx. $14.00 retail) in the first shipment, along with the other first 4 books from the collection! If I do not cancel, I will receive 8 monthly shipments until I have the entire 51-book Western Promises collection. I will receive 2 or 3 FREE books in each shipment and I will pay just $4.99 US/ $5.89 CDN for each of the other four books in each shipment, plus $2.99 for shipping and handling per shipment. *If I decide to keep the entire collection, I'll have paid for only 32 books, because 19 books are FREE! I understand that accepting the 3 free books and gifts places me under no obligation to buy anything. I can always return a shipment and cancel at any time. My free books and gifts are mine to keep no matter what I decide.

272 HCN 3070 472 HCN 3070

Name	(PLEASE PRINT)	
Address		Apt. #
City	State/Prov.	Zip/Postal Code
Signature (if under 18, a parent or guardian must sign)		

Mail to the **Reader Service:**

IN U.S.A.: P.O. Box 1867, Buffalo, NY 14240-1867
IN CANADA: P.O. Box 609, Fort Erie, Ontario L2A 5X3

* Terms and prices subject to change without notice. Prices do not include applicable taxes. Sales tax applicable in N.Y. Canadian residents will be charged applicable taxes. This offer is limited to one order per household. All orders subject to approval. Credit or debit balances in a customer's account(s) may be offset by any other outstanding balance owed by or to the customer. Please allow 4 to 6 weeks for delivery. Offer available while quantities last. Offer not available to Quebec residents.

Your Privacy—The Reader Service is committed to protecting your privacy. Our Privacy Policy is available online at www.ReaderService.com or upon request from the Reader Service.

We make a portion of our mailing list available to reputable third parties that offer products we believe may interest you. If you prefer that we not exchange your name with third parties, or if you wish to clarify or modify your communication preferences, please visit us at www.ReaderService.com/consumerchoice or write to us at Reader Service Preference Service, P.O. Box 9062, Buffalo, NY 14240-9062. Include your complete name and address.

WPBPA16R